To my beautiful son,
with love, faith and hope.

IAN EAGLETON

GLITTER BOY

SCHOLASTIC

Published in the UK by Scholastic, 2023

1 London Bridge, London, SE1 9BG
Scholastic Ireland, 89E Lagan Road, Dublin Industrial Estate,
Glasnevin, Dublin, D11 HP5F

SCHOLASTIC and associated logos are trademarks and/or
registered trademarks of Scholastic Inc.

Text © Ian Eagleton, 2023
Cover illustration by Melissa Chaib © Scholastic 2023

ISBN 978 0702 31782 8

A CIP catalogue record for this book is available from the British Library.

Printed by CPI Group (UK) Ltd, Croydon, CR0 4YY
Paper made from wood grown in sustainable forests and other controlled
sources.

1 3 5 7 9 10 8 6 4 2

www.scholastic.co.uk

CHAPTER 1

It's Monday and the first day of term when it happens.

The rumours and whispers about Mr Hamilton have been swirling around ever since we found out he was going to be our new teacher.

And of course, it has to be Paul who asks the question.

I don't like Paul. At all. He races and shoves and barrels around the playground, and he always seems to have a little gaggle of kids and a trusty sidekick following him around. Apart from being good at football, I can't think why anyone would like him. Maybe just being good at football is enough to get by? It might be because he's bigger, taller and broader than all the other boys. We learnt about the Stone Age in Year 3 with Miss Davies, and I have a theory that

Paul is still in the "caveman" phase of his evolution: someone who beats his chest, drags his knuckles and grunts a lot... Apparently he wears deodorant already (Lynx Africa, I heard). His skin is fair and his hair is always slick and gelled. Plus, he's always got the latest, trendiest shoes and clothes, and goes on constantly about how rich his mum and dad are.

It's foul.

He's foul.

Slick and gelled is the complete opposite of my hair, by the way, but I don't mind that *at all*. As if I'd restrain my lovely, wild hair!

Certainly not today! Today my hair is looking *extra* fabulous, and I am raring to go. It's been brilliant – absolutely wonderful – to not have seen Paul *once* over the summer holidays. And as annoying as it is to see him again, I'm super excited about having Mr Hamilton as our teacher.

Last year we had Miss Wilson, who seemed to spend a lot of her time barking and yelling at us all. Especially me.

Speak up, James!

Will you sit up, young man!

Stop daydreaming!

Miss Wilson was vicious! Her hair was always

tied back so tightly from her pale face that I often wondered if *this* was why she never smiled: she literally couldn't!

She used to ask me maths questions like she was firing a machine gun at me. My mind would go totally blank and I'd stutter back an answer – for some reason I always went with "seventy-three", in the unrealistic hope that it might be correct. (It actually was the right answer once, much to everyone's surprise.)

At the beginning of Year 5, there was this problem-solving task she made us do which made no sense *at all*. We had a series of addition calculations and every number linked to a letter of the alphabet. It was basically like cracking a code with maths, which sounds cool, but it was all to answer a question:

How did the candle feel when it was blown out?

And once you did all the calculations and worked them out, the answers spelled out the word "DELIGHTED".

Get it?

Well, I did not. At all. Why would a candle feel delighted if it had been blown out? Surely it would feel sad or lonely or, maybe, *here's an idea, Miss Wilson*, maybe it didn't feel anything because it was BLOWN OUT!

I did in fact get the right calculations – no, seriously – but rubbed them all out because the answer made no sense! Miss Wilson made me spend all of break and half of lunch doing all the calculations again, but I still got the same answer, which I kept thinking must be wrong.

"I ... I ... don't understand..." I finally muttered.

Obviously, now I'm in Year 6, I get the joke. Hilarious.

But I spent the rest of the year with Miss Wilson speaking to me very, very slowly, through gritted teeth. At parents' evening Dad asked Miss Wilson why I was struggling with maths and she explained what had happened very, very slowly to him too.

"Seems to me that James didn't understand a joke, Miss Wilson," said Dad with a raised eyebrow. "I'd be very happy to work with him on, say, riddles or wordplay, his witty repartee, but I hardly think his progression in mathematics should be impeded by one trivial misunderstanding."

It always makes me want to laugh so hard when Dad speaks like this, with all these fancy words,

4

because he doesn't LOOK like he would. He's a big white guy with short, cropped hair, and he's a manly man – GGRRRR! He's also got a tattoo of Mum's name on his arm, which is a bit embarrassing now because … well, they're not together any more. I once asked him if I could have a Mariah Carey tattoo and he said absolutely not, under no circumstances, EVEN when I'm eighteen.

We'll see about that!

So, excuse the tangent, there was Dad staring down Miss Wilson with his raised eyebrow, and me sat in the middle like I was at a tennis match, but instead of hitting balls, they were serving words.

Nan always says, "When you see your father raise that eyebrow, DO NOT APPROACH!"

But Miss Wilson wasn't in the slightest bit bothered by my dad's comment. She simply raised her eyebrow too (DO NOT APPROACH!) and, very quietly, very nonchalantly, whispered, "Thank you so much for your feedback, Mr Turner. As a trained and qualified teacher, I'm more than capable of assessing a child's understanding of any given topic. If you have any more" – she paused – "*opinions*, then do pass them on to Mrs Garcia."

And that was the end of that. I spent the rest of

the year dreading anything to do with maths. *It was bleak, dahhling*, as Mariah would say!

So it's nice to have a new teacher. Mr Hamilton is maybe forty years old or maybe even forty-five, but very trendy and cool. He even has a nose piercing! I feel like a nose piercing would really suit me, but I have a feeling Dad would say no to that too. And Mr Hamilton wears nail varnish sometimes, which is so glamorous! When I was really young, like six, I used to make false nails out of Blu Tack and dance around the house pointing at things. But Mum and Dad said little boys shouldn't do that to their nails, so I had to stop.

Today Mr Hamilton is wearing a deep blue shimmering shade of nail varnish and this seems to have *infuriated* Paul, by the look of disgust on his face. In fact, everything about Mr Hamilton seems to annoy Paul.

But I'm not going to let Paul bother me again this year because I already love Mr Hamilton and I *love* our new classroom. Mr Hamilton's room is quiet and calm. The display boards are all backed with hessian and everything's very simple inside, very pastel, *très chic*. It feels relaxing and grown up, like Mr Hamilton takes us seriously. (Chuck a few Mariah Carey posters up and it would be perfect!)

It hasn't all been great, though. When my dad first found out Mr Hamilton was going to be teaching me, he went into Mrs Garcia's office to "have a talk", while I waited outside. I couldn't really hear what they were saying – and believe you me, I tried – but Dad came out looking furious. He did a lot of what I call *adult tutting* that evening.

I never did find out what it was all about, but I think I now have an idea.

Because the question Paul asks Mr Hamilton is: "Mr Hamilton, do you have a wife?"

You know in old Western films when everything goes really silent and some tumbleweed rolls by? It's a bit like that.

Eventually, Mr Hamilton takes a deep breath and says, "No, I don't have a wife. I have a boyfriend – well, fiancé – called Sam. We're getting married in six weeks!"

I glance around the classroom, something strange fizzing in my stomach. Some kids look embarrassed, and some kids are whispering and giggling. Most kids don't seem to care, though, and a few are even smiling. That makes me feel … hopeful? Excited?

I'm not sure why.

But Paul's making "yuck" faces to anyone who will watch.

He's a complete cretin.

It's Harriet who breaks the silence, as usual. Her hand flies up. "How old is Sam?"

"He's forty-nine," Mr Hamilton replies, smiling a little.

"Oh, so quite old, then," says Ameera matter-of-factly.

"And what does he look like?" Harriet continues.

"Well, he has silvery-grey hair, and he's VERY tall … and…"

"And…?" Harriet says, looking at him expectantly, smiling.

"And … I think that's quite enough of that, thank you!" Mr Hamilton says, laughing. "We really need to get down to some learning!"

We all groan, which makes Mr Hamilton laugh more.

Mr Hamilton tells us that once a week we will be reading and writing poetry *for fun*. No tests, no assessments, and no marking! He says that poems are like songs that touch us deep inside and that he would like to learn more about us through our poetry: our lives, our passions, our fears and our dreams.

I scrunch up my toes in excitement and wriggle in my chair with happiness.

OK, I know that poetry isn't everyone's cup of tea, but poetry is *my thing*. Even Miss Wilson had to begrudgingly admit last year that my poems (when we did get a chance to write some) were actually quite good. I don't know what it is, but whenever I feel happy, or sad, or angry I find myself writing poems, even if it's just in my head.

Nan saves the ones I write down, saying I will be world-famous one day. In fact, it was Nan who suggested turning my poems into songs.

"You never know, James," she had said with a gleam in her eye, "maybe one day your Mariah Carey will be singing words you came up with!"

Now, if Nan were a true fan, or "Lamb", as Mariah's fans are called, she would know that Mariah is a very talented songwriter who writes her own songs. BUT Mariah might want to write a song *with* me! I could be her next songwriting partner, like Jermaine Dupri or Walter Afanasieff!

I mean: *can you even imagine?!* We belong together, Mimi!

To help us get a feeling of what Friday's poetry lessons will be like, we spend the whole of our English lesson reading poems, and Mr Hamilton asks us to use one of them as a structure to introduce ourselves to him.

I write:

I Am

I am beans on toast
I am microwavable dinners and silence
I am takeaways and unspoken questions
I have a dad who tries his best

I am I don't really know you
I am why did you leave us?
I am where are you now, and do you still care?
I have a mum who left

I am laughter, singing and dancing
I am cuddling on the sofa
I am safe when I am with you
I have a nan who means everything to me

I am Forever and Honey and Underneath the Stars
I am singing my heart out
I am One Sweet Day and Hero
I have music that makes me feel seen

OK, so the Mariah Carey references might be a bit obscure, I think – especially for an eleven-year-old kid. But she *is* a global superstar, and I feel like it's my mission to make sure everyone loves her as much as I do. Mr Hamilton did ask to get to know us, didn't he?

My love of Mariah cannot and will not be denied!

So, I leave him these little clues, like a trail of breadcrumbs in a fairy tale. As a test, I suppose.

At break, Harriet, Ameera and I try to come up with a new dance routine. I don't mean to brag, but last year we made up the best dances *ever*.

Seriously, they were the stuff of legend.

You should have seen our dance to Mariah's "Fantasy"! It was a "Five, six, seven, eight, strut, strut, dip, dip, clap, clap, shake, shake, woogah way, HEY" type of moment. We even did shows for the little kids and midday assistants, and I loved the cheering and laughter and fun. One time, one of the midday assistants, Mrs Cooke, joined in with us and it was SO funny.

So, this year, all our dances have to be even bigger and better, more extravagant! Harriet is insisting she can do a backflip because over the summer she went to one gymnastics class, but *I'm* imagining getting *loads* of kids involved in the dance and taking over the *whole* playground!

Or we could rehearse a performance for the Christmas disco and strut our funky stuff on the dance floor?

We spend break time bickering over the best way to start the dance and then, all too soon, it's back inside for maths.

I groan. *Please, no candle jokes.*

Dad says I need to try harder at maths after last year. But he also wants me to try harder at science and PE too. I'm actually not that bad at PE, I just don't like playing football at school any more. And I'm not sure why PE is so important to Dad. He once tried one of those apps that's meant to get you to run five kilometres in a month, and he gave up after three days, but there you go!

I really do try and concentrate during maths because I want to make a good impression. And Mr Hamilton explains things in quite a logical way, so I'm starting to feel better. Maybe I could be really good at maths? Maybe I'm actually a *maths genius* in disguise who just needed the right guidance to shine?

Or maybe not, because towards the end of the lesson, my mind begins to drift to Mr Hamilton's wedding. I wonder what colour suit he'll wear and if there'll be cake? *Cake is very important at a wedding,* Nan says. She says people only really go to weddings to eat cake and have a nose at what everyone's wearing.

But what *I* love the most about weddings is the dancing. Some of the other boys bomb around playing catch or hiding under tables, but I *love* to shimmy and shake on the dance floor until I'm hot and sweaty and feeling a bit delirious.

When I go to Nan's house she always has music playing, and in the summer she opens the windows so a cool breeze drifts in. We push the sofas to the end of the living room and dance.

But it's our little secret because we would never do it in front of Dad. He's not really a dancer anyway. "Two left feet," he says, with an uncomfortable shrug.

There was one wedding we went to – Auntie Kathy and Weird Bruce's – where Dad and Mum actually got up and danced, which was *so* cringe ... but it made me happy to see them smiling.

That was a long time ago, before everything changed. Now it's just me and Dad.

And he doesn't smile that much any more.

CHAPTER 2

At the end of the day, Harriet asks if any of us want to play football after school, but I tell her I'm going to my nan's, Nathan says he can't, and Joel has Scouts.

I say goodbye, put my headphones on, crank up Mariah and walk out the school gates on my own. Year 6s can walk home without supervision, so I feel very grown up as I head towards Nan's. She had a fall last month, and it was quite scary, so I promised myself that I would go and visit her after school each day. I'm very sneaky because she *thinks* I'm just coming to raid her fridge and scoff all the sweets from her special sweet tin, but really I'm there to keep an eye on her. *Mwahaha!*

It's a sunny day, and I feel a sense of relief and

quiet wash over me; at school I couldn't help but feel slightly on edge, looking over my shoulder, waiting for Paul to—

But it's going to be a good year, I tell myself. *It is! We have Mr Hamilton, and it's our last year of primary school, and I'm sitting next to Harriet.*

When Mr Hamilton said that we could choose who we sit next to – as long as we show that we can be sensible – I was so excited: Harriet, beside me for the whole year!

Harriet's been my best friend ever since playgroup. She's very short and tiny, fair-skinned and has shoulder-length hair and wide, curious eyes. We were Mary and Joseph in our first Christmas nativity, but I refused to go onstage unless I got to hold the baby Jesus doll. Harriet shrugged and handed me the baby (upside down, I might add), and we've been friends ever since. So we didn't even have to say anything when it came to picking who we would sit next to; we just knew.

Joel and Nathan chose seats in front of us. Nathan has got *so* tall and gangly over the summer holidays, like his body doesn't quite seem to know what he wants it to do. He's shaved off all his blonde hair, too, which I don't completely hate. It makes him look distinguished, and his grey-blue eyes really pop! Nathan and Harriet have been friends since for ever because their mums do yoga together. (Or is Pilates? Or Yogalates? I'm not sure.) They have spent *a lot* of time together outside of school because their parents are always round each other's houses having BBQs in the summer. When I've been there, Harriet's mum always winks and says she's having a "cheeky" glass of her "special lemonade", and we pretend we don't know what she means. But clearly we do.

Anyway, because I'm such good friends with Harriet, the three of us have sort of always come as a package.

I don't know Joel particularly well because he joined our school towards the end of Year 5 when he moved house. I volunteered as the person in Year 5 to show him around the school, and I remember feeling like it was the greatest honour *ever*. Joel has light brown skin, is stocky and has curly black hair. He has the greenest hazel eyes I've ever seen in my life. He was very quiet back then and didn't speak much to me, not at first. Then, every day, I would find out new things about Joel and like him even more. Personality-wise, he is just very chill and relaxed, and he's good at football, at maths – at everything, really! He's one of those kids who never gets involved in arguments, and everyone seems to really like him already.

Luckily, Paul chose to sit at the other end of the classroom with Jake. Jake loves animals and once brought in his stick insects from home when we were in Year 4, and I thought we were friends. Not best mates or anything, but we always chatted. But Jake hasn't spoken to me since becoming friends with Paul last year.

Oh well! His loss!

When I reach Nan's house, I can hear music playing as I walk up the pathway. The porch door is open and I hear Nan humming along to the radio. Music seems to crackle and throb throughout the house, and I instantly feel happiness spread inside me.

"Nan, it's me!" I bellow as I chuck my backpack on the floor at the bottom of the stairs and take my shoes off.

"In here, James," comes a creaky voice. I dance into the living room, and Nan gets up from her chair to spin me round, laughing. It's a throaty chuckle, full of mischief and naughtiness.

Once we stop dancing and Nan has made me a

glass of squash and I've shovelled a few chocolate biscuits in my mouth, we catch up about our days. Nan tells me how she has been into town with friends on the bus and bought new wool in the market and some second-hand books from the charity shop. She likes romance novels but will never let me read them.

I curl up next to her on the sofa and tell her all about Mr Hamilton and his wedding. As I nestle into her, I realize she feels bonier now and frail – fragile, almost. Ever since her fall she seems smaller. We don't dance together for as long now, but she says she's just happy to watch me spin and twirl. She even lets me play Mariah Carey and is learning the words to all the songs, too!

"Your hair looks lovely, by the way," she says. "And your new shoes are very swish, you handsome young man!"

"Thanks, Nan. I've gone for a natural, relaxed little look today with the hair, and I think it's working." I smile.

"Good first day, then? How's that Paul in your class?" Nan asks quietly, her brow crinkling.

"He didn't say anything to me today," I say.

I wouldn't tell anyone else about Paul, and

definitely not Dad, but Nan never makes a fuss or tells me what to do. She just listens and holds my hand.

Well, she probably hasn't made a fuss because I haven't told her *what* he says… I couldn't do that.

Because that's the main reason I hate Paul.

It started last year when he told me I sounded like a girl. That my voice was girly and silly.

Then he started whispering my name whenever he was near me:

Jaammmmeesssssssssssss.

Jammmmeesssssssssssss.

Jammmeessssssssssssssss.

It was so quiet, so insidious, and done in such a mocking, lisping way that I thought I'd imagined it at first.

But then he started to make sly comments. Nothing major. It's not like I was being beaten up and bullied or anything. It was nothing that anyone else could even hear most of the time, so there was no point making a big fuss about it. Just words like "sissy" or "poof" or "girl" or "gayboy" under his breath as he sauntered by.

I've never said anything back, and I never will. I won't give him my time or energy. I'm too busy being fabulous!

And besides, that was Year 5, and it's a new school year now. Everything will be fine. Maybe Paul's matured over the summer?

"That's good – good he's leaving you alone," Nan mutters, kissing the top of my head.

"Do I have to go home?" I ask, biting my lip. "Can I have dinner here and stay over?"

Nan sighs and says, "No, darling, not tonight. Besides, I'm not sharing my dinner with *you*!" She laughs and tickles me. "And anyway, your dad would miss you!"

"I doubt it," I mutter, feeling a tugging sensation in my chest.

Home's a bit rubbish at the moment. Yes, because of Mum and all that, but also I often catch Dad watching me now, looking worried. And a funny atmosphere fills the room whenever I mention Joel's name. Dad always makes excuses as to why he can't come round. Harriet? *Fine!* Nathan? *Brilliant!* Joel? *Oh, not tonight, mate...* Why wouldn't Dad like Joel? I can't imagine, but from the way he's been acting, sometimes I think Dad doesn't even like *me* any more.

"Don't be so hard on him, James. He's doing his best," says Nan. "Have you heard from your mum?"

"I'm not speaking to her. She keeps ringing and texting, but I don't want to talk to her."

Nan looks at me sadly but just nods.

I don't know how she feels about Mum and what Mum did; Nan never says.

Every so often, at home, I find Dad staring out of the kitchen window, and I can tell he's thinking about Mum.

Then I think maybe Mum didn't like me very much either, and that's why she left.

When I get home from Nan's, Dad is in the kitchen and there's an acrid burning smell in the house. He's wearing an apron and is surrounded by greasy cookbooks. His face is covered in flour and sweat.

Since Mum left, he's been trying to cook for us, but he's just terrible, no matter how hard he tries. A few months ago, he even started watching a TV show about cooking. He says it's to improve his "culinary skills", but I think it might be because he fancies the pretty lady chef. She's always talking about rubbing things in oil and butter. Sounds gross.

"Beans on toast again tonight, I'm afraid, mate!" He laughs apologetically. "How was school? How was maths?"

"Yeah, fine. All good," I mumble.

I trail upstairs and fling my school bag on to the floor. My Mariah Carey posters smile at me in all their glitz and glamour and shine. I close the door so Dad can't see, and then I start the music and dance and leap around my room as Mariah's voice soars and flutters.

"Turn that rubbish down!" yells Dad from downstairs. "It's time for dinner anyway!"

Every time he says that, it feels as if he's saying to me, "Everything you like is rubbish because you're rubbish!"

With a sigh, I traipse back downstairs and help set the table. We sit uncomfortably in silence for a while, me pushing my mushy beans and soggy toast around the plate and Dad chomping and chewing away.

"So, what happened at school today?" Dad finally asks. "Good first day?"

I tell him all about sitting next to Harriet and about our poetry days, and he nods along, chewing slowly. When I tell him about Mr Hamilton and Sam and how they're getting married, Dad just coughs, then clears his throat, and carries on shovelling food into his mouth.

I think that maybe he didn't hear me, so I say, "Dad ... I said Mr Hamilton is getting married to his boyfriend!"

"Oh, right, yes, lovely," he replies, trying to smile. "What did you do in maths today? And how's Nathan? Haven't seen him for ages!"

But the smile doesn't reach his eyes, and he seems distant and angry and disappointed, and I don't know why.

At bedtime, Dad comes and tucks me in. He wipes my hair from my face and gives me a kiss on my forehead. He always used to read to me, and I would snuggle into him while I listened, his rhythmic voice like a gentle lullaby. He did all the voices for the different characters and always made me feel like I'd actually jumped into the book.

But he doesn't read to me any more.

Today Mr Hamilton had set all our new class books out on the desks and let us spend ages picking and choosing a book to read at home. I chose a collection of poems about the stars and the moon, and Mr Hamilton nodded and smiled at me when he saw.

"Do you want me to read to you tonight?" I ask Dad.

It would be nice to share the book with Dad,

maybe find a connection – a way back to each other somehow.

"Not tonight, mate," says Dad.

He turns off my desk lamp and leaves me in the darkness, wondering what I've done wrong, again.

It takes me a long time to get to sleep. My mind is racing and my heart is thumping.

I wonder if Nan will be OK tonight on her own. I haven't been able to stop thinking about her fall. I'll check on her again tomorrow.

Does Dad hate me? He never seems to want to talk to me any more, not properly, and I want to tell him everything about school, about Paul, about the dances Harriet and I make up, and everything about Joel... Not just the edited version. But I know that there are some things I can't talk to him about.

Like Mum.

I don't even know where Mum is most of the time. She always seems to be travelling with work and going to glamorous places, lounging around by swimming pools with a laptop and a huge cocktail.

Not that I check her social media and stalk her on the internet. Absolutely not.

I finally go to sleep and dream of Mr Hamilton and Sam-with-the-silver-hair parachuting into the church on the day of their wedding while Mariah Carey sings a song I've written with her. Joel and I sit and watch it all – because we've been invited, obviously! Joel's wearing a velvet suit that matches his eyes. Later, there are fireworks bursting into the night sky and I'm holding a sparkler in my hand. It fizzes and shoots out hundreds of tiny, crackling lightning bolts, and the burning heat is getting closer and closer to my hand, but I never want to let go of this moment.

CHAPTER 3

"Oh, and by the way, James," says Mr Hamilton with a wink, "I liked the Mariah Carey references in your poem. Good for you!"

I feel my face go red, pleased by the compliment. It's Tuesday at the beginning of lunch and the room's empty apart from me, Mr Hamilton and Miss Clarke, our teaching assistant.

Miss Clarke is just the absolute *best*! She was our teaching assistant in Year 4 when we had Mrs Farooq. Miss Clarke has a shaved head, like Nathan, and wears a different set of dungarees each day. Sometimes they're yellow with black buzzing bees on them, sometimes they're orange and printed with flowers and sometimes they're just plain black or blue – but they're always speckled and splattered with paint.

I'm hiding in the classroom, hanging around the book corner, because it's Tuesday, which means it's a Year 6 Football Day.

And yes, it does need capital letters.

Obviously some of the kids play football every day, but a Football Day is different. Each year group in the juniors can use the field (not just the playground!) twice a week for an epic football match during lunch. For us it's every Tuesday and Friday.

Battle lines are drawn, and old feuds are reignited as teams are picked. Harriet and Paul are sworn mortal enemies on the pitch, so they always nominate themselves captains of the opposing teams. They spend the morning of a Football Day glaring at each other and gesturing across the classroom, and whispers of "You're going down!" ricochet around the playground.

The battle is ferocious and mighty. There are screams of agony, shouts of protestation and the most dramatic tackles you've ever seen in your life. There are arguments, fallouts, drama and despair, and exasperated midday assistants.

At the end of lunch, one team is crowned the winner, and some lucky captain gets ordained king or queen of the football pitch. There are cheers and all sorts of ridiculous celebrations.

And the losers? The losers face the embarrassment, the shame, *the humiliation* of being defeated.

At a lunchtime football match at school.

I don't get involved any more. I don't even watch all the drama unfold! I played a few times, but it's more Paul's thing. Best to stay away. I'll stick to dancing and let him have football!

So, even though Harriet is constantly inviting me to play, with a slap on the back and promises of looking after me on the pitch, it just seems ... unsafe.

I use the time to read instead, or write poems. Harriet says she feels bad and offers to sit with me instead of playing football, but I couldn't do that to her. I don't mind sitting on the field in the summer away from everyone else, or on a bench in the playground in autumn, reading or writing. But sometimes it feels lonely.

So today I'm hoping to be able to hang around in the classroom with Mr Hamilton and Miss Clarke. If they let me stay today, maybe I could be here for every Football Day?

"Why don't you try this one?" Mr Hamilton asks, handing me a book of shape poems. "Shape poems are surprisingly difficult to create. Maybe have a go this Friday when we do our poetry session, as a special challenge for you?" He straightens up and rubs his hands together. "Now, go on, James! Off you go outside so I can drink a vat of coffee with the other teachers."

Miss Clarke laughs. My heart sinks at the thought of going outside, but I still like her laugh – you can't help but smile when you hear it. And today she's wearing green dungarees with dinosaurs printed on them.

"Come on, Miss Clarke, time for lunch!" says Mr Hamilton, and with that he breezes out of the classroom, a box of our maths books under his arm. Miss Clarke follows him with her packed lunch.

Now that he's actually told me to go, I suppose I can't hang around in here any more. I take the book of shape poems and carry it outside. I wave to Harriet, but she's busy tearing around the pitch, a look of scary aggression on her sweaty face. She's so much smaller than all the other kids, but she's running rings around them all, and I laugh to myself that I have such a brilliant, wild, brave best friend.

Then Paul makes a rude gesture at me from across the playground, and I feel a shiver run down my spine. *It can't be happening again, can it? It's only the second day of term!*

"Hi, James!" I hear, and turn to see Mrs Gallagher walking across the playground. Mrs Gallagher always seems to be wearing gaudy floral dresses and leggings that don't match. She has pale skin and freckles. Today, her hair is scooped up in a messy bun held in place by a pencil. "Looking forward to seeing you at choir practice. It starts up again on Thursday lunchtime!"

There's a pile of books balancing in her arms, along with two coffee cups and a tired, wilted sandwich on top.

Choir practice! Now, for me, *that's* always been the best day of the week. Joel and I have been going together every Thursday lunchtime since he joined in Year 5. Harriet came to a few practices, but soon decided it wasn't really for her. This was a good decision for everyone because when Harriet's singing, it's clear that the only pitch she's thinking about is the football kind. I think Mrs Gallagher was secretly relieved too.

Mrs Gallagher always chooses the best songs: old songs that Nan recognizes when I sing them to her and some modern ones too. So far, Mrs Gallagher has resisted my efforts to convince her that singing Mariah Carey *every* week would be *amazing* ... but I'll grind her down, just you wait and see!

"Do you need any help with your books, Mrs Gallagher?" I ask innocently, a wicked little gleam in my eye.

"That's very kind, James. Actually, you could carry these for me!"

She indicates the coffee cups and the limp sandwich at the top of her pile of books – which I gently remove and hold out at arm's length – and we head towards the staffroom.

At this point, I am *frothing* with excitement. *The staffroom!* Hallowed ground! I have *never*, not once, been chosen to take something into the staffroom, or even got a peek in there. Harriet has, and she says they have a water cooler, a Jacuzzi and a wide-screen TV!

As I'm walking beside Mrs Gallagher, I wonder if the staff all like each other. Do they sit together in little cliques and groups? Do they play board games? Do they weep quietly into their lunch boxes? Does awful Miss Wilson actually eat a packed lunch, or does she merely feast on the souls of poor, innocent children?

And will Mr Hamilton *really* be glugging down a vat of coffee today? And what *is* a vat?

Most importantly, what do they *talk* about? Surely all they have to talk about is us kids?

Finally, I'm there, just outside the door, and my legs are shaking with nervous energy, my eyes darting from left to right.

"OK, we're not supposed to do this, but just pop in with me and put the things on the table at the side, OK, James?" says Mrs Gallagher.

I nod, unable to speak from sheer, giddy excitement. Then I follow her into the staffroom, juggling the mugs and her sandwich (ham and cheese from the canteen, I think – ham *and* cheese?! Wild!).

I'm so shocked at being here that I just stand and gawp around.

Oh, look! There's Miss Davies, our Year 3 teacher! There's Mrs Farooq! I give them a little wave and they wave back.

And look! There's Miss Wilson – she does *eat! And she's laughing with Mrs Garcia!*

And there's Mr Hamilton texting on his phone and sipping a huge mug of coffee on a sofa. (A sofa! How lucky are teachers?!)

I haven't spotted the Jacuzzi yet, and I'm so busy looking around, taking it all in so I can report back, that I don't notice the room has gone silent. I look up and everyone is staring at me. Actually, Miss Wilson isn't, she's *glaring* at me, and Mr Hamilton is smiling, covering his mouth with his hand, trying not to laugh.

"Erm … *thank you*, James," says Mrs Gallagher. "You've been ever so helpful. One Team Point for you."

I nod at her, smiling inanely.

"You can go now," she whispers with a grin.

Oh! Yes! Time to go!

Just wait until I tell Joel about THIS, I think as I skip out of the room.

Overheard in the Staffroom

Did you see Strictly Come Dancing last night?

Oh, he's such a pain. Never listens!

No, I'll need two sugars today, Sue!

She wants the planning in for tomorrow. Tomorrow!

GIVE ME COFFEE!

Well, I took their books home and thought,

oh, I can't be bothered.

I'll ring him at the end of the day.

I can't cope with him now.

HELP! THE PHOTOCOPIER'S BROKEN!

I TOLD him not to put the Blu Tack up his nose.

And what did he do?

Oh, they've been horrible this morning.

Is it really only Tuesday?

WE'VE RUN OUT OF GLUE STICKS!

My kids have been so adorable all morning, so well-
behaved! You should see the writing they've done.

I've completely forgotten to mark their homework

AGAIN!

Can anyone do my break duty tomorrow, please?

THE BISCUIT TIN IS EMPTY!

Well, they always behave for me!

Oh no, I couldn't, I'm on a diet. Well ... maybe one.

Mmmmmmmm! Maybe another one?

I'm so proud of them.

WHAT?! IT CAN'T BE THE END

OF BREAK ALREADY?!

"You made it into the staffroom, finally? Congratulations!" squeaks Joel, jumping on me in excitement.

"We've *all* been in the staffroom," says Nathan dismissively. Then he adds, more quietly, "Even Sandra in Year 5 says she's been in there."

"Ohhh! Sandra in Year 5!" Harriet laughs a bit too loudly. She gives Nathan a playful shove.

I laugh too because, come on, *seriously*!

We're walking home and I'm regaling everyone with the full report of my exciting escapade. The leaves are starting to turn golden, and the sunshine is hazy; everything seems to have slowed down.

"All I know," I say, whispering in an oh-so-very-serious tone, "is that Miss Wilson was eating lunch over a cauldron and nibbling on … a child's LEG!"

"Eeeewwwww! James!" Harriet squirms, punching me lightly on my arm.

Nathan huffs and puffs, but Joel bursts out laughing. It makes me happy when Joel laughs at my jokes.

We walk on for a bit, the afternoon sunshine making long shadows.

"So, all meet outside mine in fifteen minutes?" asks Harriet when we get to her road.

Nathan looks shifty and just says, "I've got spelling homework to do still."

"Loser! What about you, Joel?" asks Harriet.

"Yep, I'll be there," Joel replies.

Harriet and Joel look at me hopefully, but I say, "Not for me, I'm off to Nan's for a bit."

Joel looks disappointed for a moment, but says, "OK, see you tomorrow, then. Say hi to your nan from me!"

I leave them outside Harriet's house and head towards Nan's. On my way I pass a couple, two women. They have the CUTEST little dog, yapping at their feet.

But that's not the most interesting thing: the women are holding hands! I think how odd it is to see two ladies holding hands round here.

"So, Mr Hamilton said that I should try a shape poem this Friday when we write our poems. He said it's a special challenge for me!"

I'm sat next to Nan on the sofa, nibbling away on a chocolate biscuit. Nan had been reading the newspaper when I arrived, but she put it away as soon as I burst in through the door. We then spent some time dancing and giggling to the radio, and I taught her a short dance I've created to Mariah's diss track "Obsessed". Nan said the twerking was a bit much for her, but she gave it a good go.

Afterwards, I told her all about the Staffroom Odyssey, and now we're sat on the sofa, curled up together.

"You'll have to tell me what a shape poem is, James. We didn't do those when I was at school!" says Nan, smiling.

"What did you do at school?" I ask, sipping a cold glass of milk.

"The Three Rs – reading, writing and arithmetic," she says, chuckling.

I don't want to point out that only one of those starts with the letter "R", so I just say, "It's like you come up with a poem about something, say … a fox! And then you write a poem about a fox in the shape of a fox! But Mr Hamilton says that they *look* really easy to do, but they're actually very difficult. Which is probably why he's asked me to have a go," I add, with a smile and a cheeky shrug.

"Oh, I see!" says Nan. "And what are you going to do your shape poem on?"

"I don't know, really. I want it to be good. And Mr Hamilton says he'd like our poems to tell him all about us and what's important to us."

"Well, my love, you can only do your best. You'll think of something. Have a go on that notepad next to the sweets. And pass me a sweet while you're at it, too!"

So, for the rest of the afternoon, Nan sits reading her newspaper and occasionally tuts at "the state of the world", and I sit and write in her notepad. I make patterns and shapes out of words, and write and write, thinking about those two women and that

GORGEOUS little fluff ball of a dog I saw earlier.

These are my favourite kinds of afternoons with Nan – we just sit quietly, and neither of us feels like we have to talk. It's perfect.

<u>Thoughts of a</u>
<u>Cute Fluffy Dog</u>

Hey, you! Have you
seen my tail? Swish,
  flick, swish, flick! YEAH!
  Oh, look! A bird! Woof
  woof woof woof woof!
 Hey, you! Have you
 seen my shiny coat?
Soft and shiny, soft and
shiny! YEAH! Oh, look! A shadow!
 Yapyapyapyapyap! Hey, you! Have
 you seen my cute little nose? Twitch,
  sniff, twitch, sniff! YEAH! Oh, look!
  Food on the floor! Yumyumyumyumyum!
  Hey, you! Have you seen my strut?
   Forward,   back, turn, forward, back,   turn!
   Now   shake it! YEAH! Oh, look! A bum   to sniff!
  Sniff   sniffsniffsniffsniff! Hey, you! I think   I've done
 enough   walking for today. I'm just going to lie   down
here   while you hold hands on the sofa You   smile
at me   and I feel safe, ready to sleep, to dream,
to...   Oh, look!

CHAPTER 4

"Now, everyone! Some news. Sorry, that should be NEWS!"

It's Thursday already and Mrs Gallagher is perched on the edge of her desk in the music room. I notice she's accumulated more coffee cups. Everyone in the choir has arrived and there are giggles and whispers as kids catch up with each other. Joel and I are stood at the back, chatting about today's classroom gossip.

For the last few days, Mr Hamilton being gay seemed to be all anyone in our class talked about; everyone wanted to know more about Sam. How did they meet? What job did he do? What was his favourite food? How long had they been together? Would we get to meet him?

39

But today the gossip machine has moved on. That's because Nathan, our very own Nathan Harris, has been spotted walking around the playground with Sandra in Year 5. Could they be going out? Are they in lluuurrrvvvvvve? And, more importantly, *will they hold hands by the end of the year*?

"So," continues Mrs Gallagher, "as some of you may know, Mr Hamilton is getting married soon. His fiancé, Sam, has been into school" – she pauses dramatically – "to ask us a favour!"

A favour? From us?

There are more whispers and muttering as Mrs Gallagher lets it sink in, and everyone's looking around at each other. Maybe Sam wants us to come to the wedding, and maybe one of us (ME?!) will get chosen to throw petals, or look after the ring, or—

"Sam would like the choir to sing a song after the ceremony, after they're married! As a surprise! How exciting is *that*?" cries Mrs Gallagher, clapping her hands together.

There are gasps, and everyone in the choir begins to talk at once.

"We get to go to the wedding!" I say to Joel.

Joel nods, grinning, then puts his hand up and

says, "Mrs Gallagher, which song are we going to be singing?"

"Well, it's all been cleared with Mrs Garcia, so let me just hand out these permission slips – I need them back as soon as possible, OK? – and then we'll have a listen to the song and you can tell me what you all think…"

I shiver with delight as the music plays. The singer has a beautiful raspy voice, and it's a song about rising above all your fears and worries and being there for someone no matter what. It's gorgeous and dreamy and oh! It builds up and up and up until a full choir joins the singer, and the song seems to burst up and out into the sky. It's hopeful and romantic and happy and *perfect*. It's just like being at Nan's when the music takes me away to another place. I feel like anything could happen. This is going to be *epic*!

At the end of the day, Joel and I are walking home together. Harriet has after-school basketball practice, and – get this – Nathan is walking home with *Sandra in Year 5* today. The rumours are true!

They look quite funny together because Nathan is so tall and uncoordinated now, and Sandra is so poised and sure of herself. Her hair falls in fiery red ringlets around her face and she always seems to be glowing.

We can see them behind us and hear Nathan babbling nervously about comic books, which he loves. Sandra is smiling and nodding, but she doesn't seem particularly impressed.

Joel and I keep turning around to give him the thumbs up.

It's hilarious to torture Nathan like this, and we watch him draw a line across his throat at us as he blushes and tries to focus his attention on Sandra.

But, look, don't feel bad for him! Nathan and I have been friends *for ever*. It feels like he's always been by my side, like a brother.

That said, he hasn't been around much lately, and I haven't really seen him over the summer holidays, so it's strange seeing him now with Sandra.

"So, what did you think of the song?" Joel asks. It's colder and brisker today, and he rubs his hands together as we amble along.

I stop looking around at Nathan and turn to Joel: "I *loved* it! I mean, no, it's not Mariah Carey, but it's *beautiful*, isn't it?"

Joel laughs and says, "OK … well, what Mariah song would *you* choose for their wedding?"

I'm a little bit thrown for a moment – just a moment, mind – because, apart from Nan, no one ever talks to me about Mariah Carey. Harriet will happily throw herself around and dance to her songs, but I'm not sure she *really* gets it.

"Well…" I say slowly, considering my options, "you could go for a classic like 'All I've Ever Wanted' or 'Underneath the Stars', or maybe a more recent one like 'With You'? There's loads – loads, I tell you!"

We laugh and carry on walking.

Joel looks up at the clouds drifting across the sky and smiles sheepishly. "It's so nice Mr Hamilton's getting married. Anna in our class? Her uncles are gay, too."

I nod my head and wonder what Dad might say about it. I suppose I'll have to tell him about our secret choir surprise, but I'm worried that he might not let me go, and I *really* need a lift there, since it's out of town. I only had to *mention* Mr Hamilton and Sam getting married the other night, and look how Dad closed up and shut down.

It's like when Mum left. He shut down then too. Everything in the house seemed to turn grey and dull overnight, and even though he tries and tries so hard, it's never felt the same. I often catch him just staring at the TV or standing in front of an open cupboard door, as if he's frozen to the spot. I know he's thinking about Mum, and where she is, and why she left.

That's why I play my music every night. It gives me something to focus on and take my mind off all the thoughts and worries churning in my stomach and swirling in my head.

We slow down as we near the turning for Nan's house, and I don't know what makes me do it, but I say, "Do you want to come in and meet my nan, Joel?"

He smiles. "Yes, definitely! I'll just text Mum and let her know; she'll be fine, though. Come on, then!"

I feel nervous walking up the path. Nan's met Nathan loads of times and adores Harriet, obviously, but I just hope she likes Joel too. Really, really likes him.

Why do I care so much?

I don't! I don't!

Joel's my friend and I want her to like him, that's all.

That is all.

I call out to Nan as Joel takes his muddy shoes off in the porch (why *are* they always muddy by the way?).

But there's no answer. Something doesn't feel right, and I call out again as I fumble for my key.

"I'm in here," Nan calls out. Her voice sounds pained and small. As we push the front door open, I can see that Nan is lying on the kitchen floor, crumpled and shaking. I rush in, Joel close behind me, and collapse on the floor next to her.

I'm trying to bite back tears and she snaps, "I'm fine, James! Just a little fall. Stop staring at me and help me up!"

So, together, Joel and I heave Nan up. She's light and it feels like there's nothing of her, but she's still awkward to move, and it takes a while to get her into a proper sitting position. I scoop her up under her arms and Joel keeps hold of her legs and finally we carry her into the living room and sit her down.

"Nan, how did—" I begin, but she interrupts.

"Now, don't fuss! Honestly, I'm fine. Just need to sit for a moment. And not a word to your dad; he'll only worry! Go and pop the kettle on for me, James, and then you can introduce your friend to me!"

I feel weird leaving Joel with Nan, but as I go about making cups of tea in the kitchen, I can hear them talking and Joel's laughing. Joel is always so good at talking to everyone and making them feel at ease.

When I come back in, Nan says, "Thank you, darling. Joel and I have been getting to know each other. He said you've got a special surprise for your teacher. Sounds lovely!"

We spend the rest of the afternoon chatting. Joel and I tell Nan all about the class gossip, and she "oohhhs" and "aaahhhhs". Then we go on all sorts of tangents, and Joel ends up telling us all about the woods behind his house and how he goes there to think. (Aha! That explains the muddy shoes!)

He talks about his mum and dad and how brilliant they are, and how they take him swimming every weekend. Nan laughs because she's scared of having the water in the bath too deep, but Joel says he loves diving into the cool swimming pool and how he instantly feels weightless and peaceful.

He says his foster carers used to take him swimming – that's how he got started with it. I've always avoided asking about his family because I know he's adopted and I don't want to upset him or say something insensitive, but maybe this is Joel's way of saying, "It's OK. You can talk to me. You can ask me. This is an important part of me."

I smile to myself. We sing Nan the song we're learning in choir and she sways happily.

Just as we're about to leave, the two women I saw the other day walk past Nan's window and Nan waves enthusiastically. They smile and wave back.

"Oh, lovely couple of girls, they are! Ruth and Eliana. Ruth's the one on the left. They've just moved in a few doors down. Yappy little dog, though. I'll introduce you soon," says Nan.

"Oh! I LOVE dogs!" says Joel, beaming, and I laugh at his excitement. *Me too!*

As Joel and I walk home, the street is quiet. The autumn sun is setting and there's a balminess in the air.

"I like your nan," Joel says. "She has kind eyes."

"Yeah, she's the best." I nod, suddenly wondering if I've inherited her kind eyes too.

I feel like I've shared something special with Joel today, and it feels good.

We walk on, and after a while Joel asks, "Are you going to tell your dad about your nan's fall?"

"No, I don't think I will. She said not to," I reply, biting my lip.

Dad knows about the first fall ... but another one? *Should* I keep it a secret? Is that the right thing to do? I probably should tell Dad, but I did make a promise to Nan. And I know Dad will just put her in a care home, and she'd HATE that. And, to be honest with you, I'd hate that too. I wouldn't be able to just pop round and see her whenever I wanted.

I decide that if it happens again I'll have to tell Dad.

"I think you should tell him anyway," Joel says, turning to look at me.

"I'll think about it," I lie, avoiding his eyes. Then I stop and nod towards my house. "This is me, so I'll see you tomorrow at school."

I wave goodbye to Joel as I walk up the garden path, hoping that my decision is the right one.

CHAPTER 5

There's an eerie silence in the house when I enter. It feels damp and cold and sad. I can hear the buzz and hiss of the television and Dad calls out, "James? That you? Where have you been?"

"At Nan's again!" I say as I walk into the living room.

Dad looks tired and grizzled. He hasn't shaved for a few days and his grey joggers are dirty, covered in stains. He's sitting slumped on the sofa and looks exhausted. Every day the living room seems to get messier and messier.

"Oh, right." He nods without looking at me. "Just text me if you're going to be late again, OK? There's some stuff going on at work at the moment and I'm needed for extra shifts. I just need to know what you're doing and where you are."

What's going on at work, I wonder, and why is he suddenly so obsessed with where I am? I want to ask if everything's OK, but I just say, "Sorry ... Joel and I were chatting to Nan and we lost track of time. Joel was telling us all about his parents, and how they take him swimming, and it was *so* cute, and..."

There's a flicker of something across Dad's face, but before I can think about it, it's gone. *What was I thinking? Rule Number 1: don't mention Joel!*

"Maybe you shouldn't be going to your nan's every day after school. I can check on her in between my shifts," Dad says.

"But—" I start, but Dad has raised his eyebrow. DO NOT APPROACH.

"Go on, then, mate. Upstairs, and wash your hands before dinner. I'll order us a takeaway or something. And have you got any homework? Spelling? Times tables?"

"No, not today," I mutter, feeling like I've been shut down, silenced. Dad doesn't seem to care or want to hear what I have to say. I trudge up the stairs, frustrated. It's like there's a stone in my stomach, hard and heavy.

Fine, then! I won't tell him about Nan, or about choir practice and our surprise.

I fall on to my bed and close my eyes. *What's the point?*

"The poems we are going to share today all have a theme of celebrating people who are important to the poet," says Mr Hamilton at the front of the class. "So afterwards I'd really like us – I'm going to be writing too – to craft some poems about people who are special to us."

He has his hair tied up in a bun today, and is wearing a bright shirt, cream trousers and a pair of loafers. His nail varnish is pale turquoise today. He looks very stylish.

It's Friday, the day we get to read and write our own poems. I am *buzzing*.

"Now, remember, the poems you write today are for you. No one else! I will have a read of them if you want, but I won't be marking them, and if you'd prefer me NOT to read them, that's fine too, just say so. OK, off you go!"

He nods at us and smiles.

I've been practising shape poems all week. I feel like it's a little personal challenge from Mr Hamilton, and I want to do him proud. My bedroom is covered in notes and ideas, pictures and patterns.

We spend the first part of the lesson immersed in the poems Mr Hamilton provides as inspiration. Harriet and I take it in turns to read them to each other, and we talk about what we like about them and if anything is confusing us.

And then it's over to us to write! This is going to be so much fun! Plus, it will be GREAT practice for me because someday I'm going to be a songwriter working with Mariah Carey.

Harriet says she's going to write about her baby brother Ellis, and Ameera is going to write about Miss Clarke. I wonder if Nathan will write about one of his superheroes. Or … maybe Sandra in Year 5?

Who should I write about? I wonder.

Nan? Dad? Harriet? Nathan?

Mum?

No, not Mum.

After fifteen quiet minutes have passed, I still haven't written anything. Then Mr Hamilton announces he's written his poem like a conversation.

"I know you've all been whispering about me and want to know more about Sam." He smiles at us, his eyebrows raised jokingly. "Teachers hear the playground gossip too, you know! So, this poem is for you."

He displays his poem on the interactive whiteboard:

What's His Name? by Mr Hamilton

"What's his name?" they ask.
"Sam," I answer.

"Tell us more!" they demand.
"He likes rugby. A lot," I say, and smile.
"I usually do some gardening or read my book
while he watches it. Sometimes he goes with his
dad to watch our local team play."

"Tell us more!" they yell.
"Hmmmm… He's a TERRIBLE cook.
Absolutely awful! I do all the cooking at home
because he burns everything! He once cooked
for some friends and it was so BAD we had
to order in a takeaway!"

"More! What else?" they beg.
"He's VERY untidy. His office upstairs is a complete
mess. He says he knows where everything is and that
I need to CHILL OUT! He NEVER washes up.
He just leaves everything in the sink!"

"MORE!" They giggle.

"At the weekend, he goes running with our dog.
I used to go with Sam, but I'm REALLY slow,
so he takes the dog with him instead.
He says running helps clear his mind."
"YOU'VE GOT A DOG?!" they shriek.
"What's his name?"

I smile. It's funny and sweet, and I like learning more about Mr Hamilton and Sam.

Everyone settles back into their writing. Mr Hamilton stops by and whispers, "Looking forward to your shape poem, James!"

I nod nervously and take a deep breath. This should be a piece of cake – then why am I suddenly feeling so blank?

Joel turns around and sees my worried face. "You OK?" he whispers. "What are you writing about?"

"Not sure yet," I reply. "Just trying to think!"

Joel looks at me with his crooked grin and his whole face lights up. "It'll be brilliant, don't worry!"

His green, green eyes twinkle for a brief second before he turns back around and continues furiously writing.

I pick up my own pen and begin.

<u>Someone Special</u>

Your
eyes are
stars which twinkle
in the darkness; my
guide through the night-time gloom.
When they shine, I am myself. I feel complete.
They lead the way
and fill me with
hope.

Mr Hamilton is supporting Anna, Harry and Ohrim in the Book Corner, discussing their ideas and recording key words and spellings for them.

Miss Clarke is wandering around the classroom, occasionally stopping and giving advice. She stands over me and says, "How are you getting on? Can I take a peek, James?"

But I begin to sweat and shake my head.

Please no. Not this one.

So, Miss Clarke just nods and smiles at me and wanders away to help Rafe, who is waving his hand around desperately. He's decided to write about his pet hamster.

Before I know it, the lesson is nearly over. I feel proud of my poem, but I'm not sure who it's about, not really. It was just ... a feeling I had.

Some of the others read their poems out to the class.

I don't. Definitely not with my gay-sounding voice.

And besides, I don't know why, but *this* poem seems special, quiet, private.

As we get ready for break, I shove it in my drawer. I get the sense that if I shared it, I'd be in trouble.

Something about it feels wrong.

CHAPTER 6

"Did you do the maths homework?" Jake asks Paul. We're lined up outside class after break, waiting for Mr Hamilton.

"Urgh, yeah," moans Paul scornfully. "It was SO gay, wasn't it?"

"Sooooooo gay!" agrees Jake.

Ah. Here we go, I think to myself, feeling my heart give way slightly.

Now, clearly, Paul doesn't mean that the homework is actually gay. He means rubbish. Loads of kids have started saying it, not just Paul. Everything's "soooooooo gay" because being gay is apparently uncool, pathetic, weird, abnormal.

I wonder how Mr Hamilton would feel if he heard someone from our class say it. But everyone knows not to say something like that in front of the grown-ups.

Suddenly I feel Paul's hot breath behind me and my stomach lurches. My shoulders immediately hunch over like I'm shrinking and my hands clench. It feels horrible to have someone so close to me. My heart is thumping and I freeze.

He kicks the back of my heels ever so lightly … and keeps doing it. Again and again.

Where's Harriet? She should be standing next to me!

"Nice poem, by the way, Jamessss…" Paul whispers into my ear.

His voice is low and menacing, and that knot in my tummy just won't go away. Did he really find it? When? How? Has he been through my desk drawer at break time? I feel burning anger that Paul might have looked through my things and doesn't even feel like he has to hide it. That I'm so insignificant and worthless that he thinks he can do whatever he wants to me.

That poem is mine. It's private.

"Who's it about, eh? Your little girlfriend Harriet? Is it Harriet?" He sniggers as he jabs a finger into my back.

I can't move, can't turn around to face him. I keep staring forward, hoping someone will see. But Harriet and Joel and Rafe are at the front of the line talking loudly about football.

"Or it could be for your boyfriend, Joel? Maybe I should tell him about it…"

Just then Mr Hamilton appears, rushing along the corridor with a stack of paper wobbling and balancing in his arms. "Sorry, 6H! The photocopier broke just as I was photocopying today's maths work. Always the way!" Mr Hamilton laughs, looking slightly harassed and sweaty.

Miss Clarke isn't with us all the time, as she works in other classes too, and Mr Hamilton is always forgetting things when she's not around to organize him.

"In you go, in you go! Harriet, Rafe, Joel – in pairs, please! Aren't you meant to be with James, Harriet?"

"Sorry, Mr Hamilton," says Harriet as she rushes back next to me. "What's wrong?" she whispers when she sees my nervous face.

"Nothing," I mutter sharply, but I still feel sick and my heart is hammering as we filter into the classroom.

It's starting again.

*

I can't concentrate for the rest of the day.

I'd convinced myself that all of this with Paul would just fizzle out over the summer holidays. That I'd come back better and brighter than ever, ready for Year 6 – my *Emancipation of Mimi* era, to put it in Mariah terms. I'd told myself that Paul would just leave me alone.

But the thought of him rifling through my drawer... I would never do that to someone else.

I try to check my drawer at lunchtime, but Mr Hamilton shoos me out, and the midday assistants won't let us back into the classroom during our lunch break. For the whole afternoon in class, I'm too afraid to turn around or move in case Paul is watching me. I can feel his eyes burning into my back from across the classroom, and I sit on my hands to stop them from shaking.

I shouldn't have written the poem. It was reckless. Completely my fault.

It was just what I was feeling at the time! Nothing special.

What if Paul tells Mr Hamilton, or my dad, and I'm told off? What if he tells the whole class that I've been writing love letters to Joel?

And where is the poem, anyway? Is it still in

my drawer? Maybe Paul has made a photocopy of it somehow and given it to everyone in the class. Everyone in the school!

I'm sure Jake was looking at me strangely earlier...

Nan says I'm a worrier. Sometimes my thoughts just run away from me and I get anxious and nervous. I feel like everyone's looking at me, and my thoughts tumble away, and—

"James? Are you listening?" I look up and Mr Hamilton is smiling at me, but he looks concerned.

"Erm, yes. Sorry..." I feel my face flush and my ears start to burn.

"And so, as I was saying, there are so many important people all throughout history who never get spoken about in schools. Who here learnt about Christopher Columbus, or Florence Nightingale, or Ernest Shackleton in Key Stage One?"

Half the class put their hand up, not quite sure what Mr Hamilton is getting at; the other half probably don't remember what we did yesterday, let alone in Year 2. I don't put my hand up – Paul might say something about my voice if I get called on.

"What about Harvey Milk? James Baldwin? Sylvia Rivera? Virginia Woolf? Catherine Duleep Singh?" Mr Hamilton continues.

We look blankly at him.

"I know when I've taught World War Two, for example, we've looked at evacuation and the home front, but never really looked at someone like Alan Turing, who was a gay man involved in codebreaking."

Gay, gay, gay, gay, gay—

Stop it, James! You don't need to do Paul's work for him.

"In fact, there are lots of people, not just from the LGBTQ+ community…"

There are a few sniggers as he says all this, but Mr Hamilton ignores them and carries on.

"… who have done amazing things throughout history."

Why is Mr Hamilton talking about gay people and people in the BLT community?

Oh, make it stop! I shrink into my seat. My face is burning.

Paul's going to say something about my poem any minute now. He'll say, *"Oh, James knows all about the gay community! You should read his poem!"*

"Now, in English we're going to be looking at biographies and non-fiction for the next few weeks," Mr Hamilton says, "and I thought it would be interesting if I gave you different significant people from history, so you can research their achievements and lives."

"Oh, oh! Mr Hamilton!" Ameera's hand shoots up.

Mr Hamilton nods at her.

"Could we do some presentations and create posters about them and draw pictures of them?" Ameera is really good at drawing, so she's always trying to make everything an art project.

"That sounds like a nice idea. We are actually going to be doing a presentation as part of this unit of work. We'll also be developing our writing skills by crafting biographies, so there's no reason why you couldn't illustrate your biographies or use photographs or artwork in your presentation."

Ameera rubs her palms together and says, "Yyyyyyeeeeessssssssssss!"

Mr Hamilton is beaming, and everyone seems intrigued or excited.

But not me.

I'll have to speak.

In front of people.

The boy with the big, gay, girly voice is going to have to present in front of the class.

In front of Paul.

"OK, so you can work with whoever you want to," Mr Hamilton says.

There's a groan from some children, and I'm surprised when Harriet practically leaps on poor Nathan. He looks slightly mortified when she squeals, "Nathan! You and me, buddy! Mate! You and me, yeah?"

Why would Harriet choose Nathan and not me?

"Erm … excuse me, Harriet!" I say tartly.

"It's good to mix things up, James! Come on, Joel! Swap with me so I can sit next to Nathan!" Harriet says as she jumps up, not giving Nathan time to reply or agree.

What is going on? Harriet's meant to be my best friend?

Inside Harriet's School Bag

1. A note from your mum to say "Sorry, we haven't done the grammar homework. Ellis kept us awake all night and we're exhausted, and I've no idea what subordinate clauses are. Harriet will do the homework at the weekend, I promise."

2. A sponge football with your name on it. Paul once stole your football in Year 2 and told everyone it

was his. So, you hit him and have always brought your own football in ever since then.

3. Books by Katherine Rundell. You LOVE her books. You like that girls can have adventures on the rooftops of Paris and explore dangerous jungles and lead revolutions in snowy Russia.

4. A crumpled photo of baby Ellis when he was in your mum's tummy. You showed EVERYONE and went on for weeks about how you were going to be a big sister.

5. A cinema ticket from my eleventh birthday. Nathan and Joel were still on holiday, so it was just you and me. We snuffled popcorn, laughed, gossiped and got told off for being too noisy. It was the perfect day.

6. Your Reading Diary. We're meant to write down every time we read in it, but you just write down all the scores of any football matches you've played at lunch. Mr Hamilton doesn't seem to mind.

7. A picture of Jack Grealish that Ameera drew for you ages ago. Apparently he joined Aston Villa when he was SIX YEARS OLD. Your dream is to play football in the Women's Super League.

8. A hairband wrapped around your glasses case, so you can tie your hair up before you THRASH everyone at football.

65

9. A Post-it note from your mum telling you how amazing and cool and strong you are. She used to write one every day for you, but you haven't found one in your bag for a while.

10. A note for Nathan. You won't tell me what's on it.

Joel gets up and swaps places with Harriet. He's relaxed, not fazed by any of it at all. He smiles at me and whispers, "Looks like it's me and you, then, eh?"

I stick my thumbs up at him, which I immediately see is a very weird and extremely uncool gesture.

What is wrong with me? *It's just Joel!*

Joel with the very green eyes. And curly black hair. And green eyes. And we're working together. Which is fine. Because we walk to school together now. And go to choir together, don't we?

Stop being such a weirdo, James!

It'll be fine. It'll be fine, I tell myself.

"So, everyone, here comes the fun bit!" Mr Hamilton laughs.

I raise my eyebrows. Usually when teachers say that something is going to be fun, it is most certainly not fun.

"I've written down the names of different famous people who I think might interest you, and I'm just going to go ahead and hand them out randomly to you!"

Please no one gay. As long as I don't have to talk about anyone gay. Can you imagine! The kid who's being called "poof" and "gayboy" having to talk about a gay person.

No way. That really would be the nail in the coffin. The end of it all.

Paul puts his hand up, and, without even waiting for Mr Hamilton to acknowledge him, sulkily says, "But what happens if we get someone we don't like or don't want to research?"

Mr Hamilton smiles at him, but I bet he's thinking, *You annoying brat! Why don't you just zip it?*

Maybe that's just me.

Instead he says, "Well, the project is really about your presentation skills and writing an engaging biography. I don't want you to spend for ever choosing someone. Plus, I'd really like you to discover some new famous faces…"

Paul looks unimpressed, but Mr Hamilton continues and says, "So, I'm going to say that you're in Year 6 now, and you'll just have to accept who you're given and make the most of it. OK?"

Boom! Take that, Paul!

Paul looks annoyed now, but just nods and mutters, "Yeah, fine…"

And with that, Mr Hamilton begins to hand out the names of the people we're going to be learning about: Maya Angelou, Nelson Mandela, William Shakespeare, Nellie Bly, Percy Lavon Julian, Violet Jessop, Annie Edson Taylor, Yuan Longping and so on.

Please let us get Mariah Carey! I think desperately to myself.

I'm only half joking.

"Here you go, chaps." Mr Hamilton smiles. "You've got…" He pulls a folded piece of paper from an empty lunch box, and it's like waiting for the results of one of those talent shows on TV when the lights dim and there's a dramatic drum roll.

I wait.

And wait.

Please no one gay.

"You've got … Marsha P. Johnson!" exclaims Mr Hamilton, grinning.

Joel and I look at each other.

Who?

Maybe she's a singer or a famous gymnast? Oh! Or an acrobat who rides elephants *while* singing? Or a scientist who foils alien attacks? Or maybe she's somehow related to Mariah Carey and I can basically just write all about Mariah?

I breathe a sigh of relief, though, because it's not that Alan Churning guy, the gay one, so it's all good! Phew.

"OK, that's everyone with a famous person now," says Mr Hamilton eventually. He's returned to the front of the class. Ameera is trying to swap with someone who has Frida Kahlo, but Miss Clarke won't have any of it.

"So, we'll have some time to research our famous people over the next few weeks while we prepare for our presentations. But I just wanted to give you your names before the end of the day so you can be thinking about them and maybe do some research if you wish!"

"I've never heard of Marsha P. Johnson," Joel says to me.

"I've decided she's a circus acrobat who sings while riding elephants and then saves the world from alien attacks." I nod seriously.

Joel laughs and says, "This is going to be fun AND we get to work together finally!"

I smile nervously at him.

Maybe this could all work out after all.

CHAPTER 7

At the end of the day, when the five-minute timer is on for us to tidy up, I feel a weird mix of emotions. Firstly, I'm excited about working with Joel and interested to find out about Marsha P. Johnson; I wonder who she is and what her achievements are. However, I am also a teeny, weeny, just-a-little-bit annoyed that Harriet didn't want to work with me. But that's fine.

Not a problem. At all.

But sitting beneath all of these emotions, still twisting my stomach into knots, is the feeling of fear and apprehension that has sat with me all afternoon: what if Paul really has read my poem? I haven't had a chance to check and see if it's still there.

So, I quickly sneak over to my drawer. If Mr

Hamilton asks, I can say I am putting away a pencil, or heard a noise from my drawer and was investigating, or that I thought I saw a mouse scurry into my drawer, or that—

Well, maybe I'll just say I was putting my pencil away.

If anyone even asks, that is. I mean, it's not that strange to be clearing stuff up and putting things in our drawers.

Stop being weird, James!

My heart is thudding violently in my chest. I almost don't want to open the drawer. I hear Nan's voice in my head – *If worrying did any good, I'd do it all the time* – and decide that quick is the best way to do this. Like ripping off a plaster. I grip my drawer and yank it open…

It's there!

I lean in slowly to inspect it.

It's fine! There's nothing on it! I was expecting it to be crumpled up or torn into pieces. Or for it to have deep pencil marks gouged into the paper.

I had thought it might have *that word* scrawled across it.

GAY.

But there's nothing on it. It's sitting in my drawer,

blasé, not a care in the world! And that's a good thing, isn't it?

Isn't it?

Then why do I still feel sick?

It's the not knowing, that's what it is. If it had been defaced in some way, then at least I'd know that Paul had been in my drawer and read it. But now I don't know. He *could* have read it. I'm just left wondering.

"I'll catch up with you all later," I say to Joel, Harriet and Nathan, who are already lining up to leave. Nathan doesn't respond because he's talking to Jake, and easy-going Joel just nods. Harriet looks confused for a moment but doesn't push it, and eventually they all file out, until I'm left alone in the room.

I go back to my drawer and feel so, so stupid to have let this happen. There must be something wrong with me. There's a throbbing in my temples and I can feel hot tears pricking at my eyes. But I will not cry. Not over Paul.

I can deal with this. I can. Come on, James! Think!

So, I grab the poem and race across to the paper recycling bag in the corner of the room and rip, rip, rip it into tiny pieces. I have to get rid of the evidence!

Because it does feel like evidence, like it reveals

a secret part of myself that I'm too ashamed to face. I watch the paper flutter into the bag, like snow, but still feel a tightness in my chest. I kneel down and stuff the fragments further into the bottom of the bag.

Just then, I hear a noise and stand up, spinning round, guilt splashed across my face.

It's Paul.

Where has he come from?

He stands by the classroom door, sneering and smirking at me. "Everything OK, Jamessssssssss?" he asks, drawing out the end of my name in an effeminate, theatrical way.

I can't look at him.

He is like a wolf, a snarling, snapping predator, and I am his prey. Weak and afraid.

I quickly cross the room, into the cloakroom, to collect my coat and bag. He watches me, eyes glinting, and slowly follows, sauntering into the cloakroom, humming to himself.

Humming is usually a happy sound, but Paul's humming sounds threatening. I can feel myself getting hotter and my skin is itching as I fumble to pack my bag, dropping my spelling book and book of poems on the floor. As I go to pick them up, Paul's foot lands on them, and I'm on the floor with him towering over me.

I hate myself. I should stand up, or shout at him, or push his foot off.

He grinds his dirty shoe into my spelling book and then kicks it so it skitters across the floor.

I can't bear the idea of looking up at him, and it's as if I can't move.

He kneels down so his face is in mine. And then he does something which surprises me.

He laughs.

He laughs and laughs.

"Only mucking about, Jamessssssss! Don't look so frightened, you big GAY!" Suddenly his voice becomes really quiet and low. "I'll see you next week."

And then he's gone.

I release my breath in a long sigh and wrap my arms around my knees so that I'm tucked up tight in a ball on the floor. My hair is plastered to my forehead and my school shirt is clammy and stuck to my back. I sit, shaking, until my breathing begins to return to normal.

"James! What are you still doing here?" Mr Hamilton is standing in the doorway with a puzzled look on his face. "Is everything OK?"

My voice doesn't sound like my own as I say, "Yeah, fine. Sorry, I just dropped my books out of my bag."

Mr Hamilton looks at me for a moment, as if he wants to say something, but then shakes his head.

"Well, I'll walk you out to the school gates and make sure you get off OK."

I nod. It's all I can manage.

My throat feels dry, and I just want to go to Nan's and sit quietly with her. I follow Mr Hamilton out of the classroom and walk through the deserted school. The cleaners have started to arrive, and I can see Mrs Gallagher marking books in her classroom as we walk by. We head outside into the playground and towards the school gates.

Paul is just leaving with his childminder, who's late again. He turns and shouts, "Bye, Mr Hamilton, have a good weekend! See you, James!" His smile is sickly sweet, but his eyes flash with loathing.

Mr Hamilton waves, watches them leave, and then says, "Are you sure you're OK, James? If you want to have a chat about anything…"

"I'm fine, honestly," I say quickly. "I should get going."

He nods but doesn't seem convinced.

I don't want to speak to him about it.

I don't want to tell anyone what Paul calls me.

I don't want to have to say *that word* out loud.

Finally, Mr Hamilton says, "OK, then, James. I'll see you on Monday. Take care."

I don't turn around, but I can feel Mr Hamilton watching me as I leave.

CHAPTER 8

As I turn down Nan's road, I start to feel easier, less anxious.

Just forget about it, I tell myself. *So, Paul called me gay. It's a ridiculous comment from a ridiculous, horrible boy.*

It's fine. I am fine.

But what if … what if Paul sneaks back into the classroom and pieces together my poem?

He might show people.

He might show it to my dad, or Joel, or Harriet…

And why me? How has he decided I'm gay? What is it about me?

I'm so lost in thought that I nearly walk into Joel, who is standing outside Nan's house looking at me, worried.

"All right, mate?" he asks.

I nod, again. I feel like I've spent a lot of time nodding today. I do feel better seeing him, though. "I'm GREAT!" I say a little too loudly.

"I just wanted to make sure you were OK," Joel says. "You didn't seem OK at the end of class. Is it about working with me on the project?"

"No, no, not at all! I'm fine. Just … Paul being … Paul."

Joel shakes his head angrily. "He's a loser. I don't know why people put up with him. Seriously, mate, just ignore him. I'll meet you outside yours on Monday morning, yeah?"

I smile at Joel and feel my tummy fizz. He's a good friend.

"Cool," I say. "I'd better go. I can see my nan snooping on us through the window."

Joel laughs and turns around and waves at Nan, who quickly drops the net curtains.

I say goodbye to Joel and fire off a quick text message to Dad:

Just popping in 2 C Nan. Be bk by 5.

Dad's kept to his word and has started checking in on Nan between his shifts. Nan always says what a good son he is, and it's weird thinking of him as anything other than my dad.

When I walk into the living room, though, I know immediately that something's wrong. Nan has her eyes closed and is sitting on her armchair holding the right side of her chest.

"Nan? What's happened?" I ask, kneeling down by her side.

"Oh, nothing, love, don't worry about me. I had some pains this morning, but I'm fine, just a bit tired. Don't look at me like that, I'm fine!"

I screw my face up. "Nan, this is happening more and more. I'm worried."

I should have told Dad. I need to tell Dad.

"Stop fussing! I'll just…" She goes to get up, but winces and holds her hip. "Go on, go and put the kettle on. No dancing for me today, though… Oh, how is your choir song coming on for the wedding?"

I know she's changing the subject and sigh, but her face is defiant, daring me to push any further. When Nan decides she doesn't want to talk about something, that's it. Mum always did say that Nan and Dad are as stubborn as each other.

Later, I sit and watch Nan reading the newspaper, and wonder again if I'm doing the right thing by not telling Dad about the falls, and now these chest pains.

Maybe she *should* be in a care home?

But then everything would be different.

I should tell Dad. I should.

What happens if she has a fall and someone isn't around to help her?

But I don't want to break her trust.

Urgh! Growing up is so hard!

I take the notepad from the side table, and begin to write:

<u>Recipe to Make a Nan</u>

A handful of kindness
A sprinkle of mischief and laughter
A slice of patience and acceptance
A vat of pure love
And a pinch of stubbornness.

As I walk home, the lights of the houses along Nan's road are coming on, bathing the street in a warm orange glow. At any other time, it would feel comforting and cosy, but not tonight.

Tonight, I just feel sick.

What do I do about Nan? I have to tell Dad. I have to tell someone.

I'm so deep in thought, a storm of confusion brewing inside, that I don't see Ruth and Eliana until it's too late and I practically walk straight into them. The cute-little-fluffy-rat-dog yaps and barks at me.

I reach down to stroke her and she tries to lick my face. So adorable!

"Stop your woofing," Eliana says, just as Ruth says, "You're James, aren't you? Your nan's told us ALL about you!"

"Yes ... erm ... hey!" I say, trying desperately not to look up at them.

They're holding hands.

Gay.

Gay.

Gay.

What if Paul sees me with them?

"Hi, James! Nice to meet you. I'm Ruth, and this is Eliana."

Ruth is wearing a tracksuit and joggers. She has dark brown skin and looks like she's full of energy and spends all her time running. Eliana has tanned skin and chestnut-brown hair. She seems softer and quieter. She reminds me of Joel.

"How's your nan doing?" asks Ruth. "We popped round the other day to introduce ourselves and ended up staying for two hours, just eating biscuits and chatting. Great lady!"

And it's then that I blurt it out, and I have no idea why: "She keeps having falls, and she's hurt her hip, I think, and her chest hurts, and she's told me not to tell ANYONE."

I immediately feel guilty. *Nan is going to kill me for telling them*, I think.

Ruth and Eliana look at each other for a beat, and Eliana looks uncomfortable.

But Ruth crouches down in front of me so I have to look in her eyes, and says quietly, "That must be really tough. Would it be OK with you if we kept an eye on her? I can pop in tomorrow morning before work?"

I drag my eyes away from Ruth and look at the ground. "Thank you ... thank you," I say, breathing a sigh of relief.

The cute-little-fluffy-rat-dog starts yapping at me again, and Ruth says, "Right, James, we'd better walk this little madam before she gets really angry! We'll pop into your nan's tomorrow, OK?"

Eliana smiles at me and gives a short, sharp yank on the little dog's lead (SO CUTE!!) and they head off down the road.

I feel the ache in my chest lift slightly.

When I get home, the house is silent. There's a note from Dad on the fridge that says, *Been called into work, be back by 8 p.m. Money for takeaway on side*.

I sigh. Another takeaway. It was exciting at first – I mean, what kid doesn't love fast food and takeaways? But now it's just getting boring.

Dad's doing his best, though; I know he is.

And anyway, Dad working late is a relief. I kind of just want to be on my own for a while. It's been a day.

Am I a terrible grandson? Am I being selfish?

And what about that poem? It's got me into so much trouble.

And what am I going to do about our secret choir surprise and Mrs Gallagher's permission slip?

And is Nathan OK? Is he being weird with me, or am I just imagining things?

And—

Suddenly, my phone rings and its loud shriek abruptly stops my cascading thoughts. I fumble in my pocket for it and immediately recognize the number.

It's Mum.

Not now. Not now, please. I press "Cancel" and turn the phone off.

I can't face speaking to her, not today.

I walk upstairs and collapse on to my bed.

As I close my eyes, I see Paul's face looming over me; I am back in the cloakroom, and I am frightened.

I did nothing.

So pathetic and useless. I should have shoved him, or told Mr Hamilton, or told Nan, but I feel ashamed and I don't know why. Maybe he's right about me? Maybe I have a girly voice, and I'm *that word*, and I deserve it. Perhaps this is just what happens to kids like me?

I climb under the bedcovers in my school uniform and listen to Mariah Carey in the gathering gloom. There's a song she sings that I love called "Outside". Mum and I used to listen to it together. Once, when I was feeling fed up, Mum performed it for me, using a wooden spoon as a microphone and dramatically mimicking all of Mimi's gestures and hand movements, and I couldn't help but laugh. The song's about feeling like you never fit in and never feeling good enough.

That's me completely. I never quite get what people

want from me, and I spend a lot of time worrying and feeling anxious.

I let the music swoop and soar throughout my room, and hope that tomorrow will be a better day.

CHAPTER 9

"How's your project going, then?" Harriet asks at break time the following Monday. She's experimenting with pigtails today. A bold choice.

After a quiet Saturday, I had begun to relax, but the dread kicked in again on Sunday night and now I'm back on full alert. As soon as I came into class this morning, I checked the paper recycling bag.

It was empty.

I *know* that it's been emptied by one of the cleaners, I know that, but the thought that Paul might be showing everyone the pieces of my poem still haunts me.

"Heelllloooo! Earth to James! How is your project going?" Harriet repeats, waving her hands in front of my face.

"Erm … I think Joel's been doing some research on it, but we haven't really started yet," I mutter non-committally.

I hope Paul doesn't hear me speaking about it.

And I hope he doesn't find out who Marsha P. Johnson is.

Because I have.

And it is not good for me. At all.

I used Dad's laptop last night to start some research on her. But as I read about Marsha's life, my skin began to prickle.

Words like *GAY RIGHTS, DRAG QUEEN, GENDER-NONCONFORMING, TRANSGENDER, GAY, GAY, GAY, GAY, GAY, GAY* popped up and seemed to dance all over the screen.

I could feel myself getting hotter and hotter and so panicked: *No, no, no!* As if Paul needs any more ammunition to use against me! The kid with the gay voice who's a great big sissy is learning about a *gay activist*? Oh, he *must* be gay, then!

And what if Dad saw those words? What would he say?

It was all too much, so, heart pounding, I deleted my internet browsing history and slammed the laptop shut.

I mean, really? Why? Why, out of all the people

could have been given, do we have to get her? Did Mr Hamilton plan this? No, he can't have!

Dad will find out.

Paul will find out. Maybe he knows already.

"Well, Nathan and I are doing Emily Davison," Harriet continues. She's bouncing on the spot and smiles happily at me before carrying on. "I wanted Maya Angelou, but Emily Davison sounds quite cool. Apparently, Mum says she fought for women to get the right to vote and was really brave! Something happened with a horse, I think, too, but I can't remember now. Maybe she rode around on one whacking men on the head? Ha! Can you imagine!"

Harriet bursts out laughing and starts galloping around the playground in a circle, pretending to whack the boys over the head.

But when she returns, I just nod and say, "Cool!" with as much energy and enthusiasm as I can muster.

Harriet stops leaping and twirling. She looks me dead in the eyes. "James, are you OK? You seem a bit…"

"I'm fine!" I say sharply, and Harriet winces.

"OK… Anyway," she says, "I'm going to go and walk by Paul and give him the evil eye. It'll psych him out for tomorrow's football match…"

And with that she's gone, and I'm left in the playground feeling like a horrible person and terrible friend, again.

On Tuesday at break time, I am choreographing a dance with Ameera, Summer and Harriet to Mariah's "Loverboy".

Yes, the dance is a bit outlandish.

Yes, it might be a tiny bit inappropriate for ten- and eleven-year-olds, but we are having so much fun!

The dance is fast-paced, with a "strut, strut, shrug, shrug, dip, dip, shake, shake" moment. Unfortunately, after a lot of tries, none of us can get it totally right. We end up freestyling, and I spin and twirl Harriet round and round, and soon we are howling with laughter. When we stop, we are both doubled over, clutching at our stomachs.

Eventually we stop laughing and I look up and see that Paul is watching me. He's on the opposite side of the playground with a group who's been playing Bulldog. (It'll get banned again, you wait and see. Every week it gets banned because it's too rough, and every week Paul and his friends invent a shiny new game which is basically Bulldog, but called something different and is *definitely not* Bulldog.)

Paul is staring at me with a look of satisfaction. Then his lip curls in disgust and he smirks at me and waves, his wrist limp. He blows me a kiss and runs off laughing.

What was I thinking? Drawing attention to myself like that?

Paul seems to be everywhere I go at the moment, like some kind of ominous, threatening shadow. When we are led out to assembly, he checks if I'm alone, then moves so he's behind me and lightly kicks the back of my feet and whispers, "Jamessssssssss" over and over.

It's hardly something I can tell anyone about, especially not Mr Hamilton or Dad.

Can you imagine? "Oh, someone's whispering my name." Poor old me!

It sounds ridiculous. Best to ignore it and not give him what he wants, which is a reaction. I am better than that. It takes all my strength to ignore him, but I do it. I look forward as I walk, never turning round.

But as much as I pretend it's not happening to me and that it's not really a big deal, it is. I'm not sleeping very well, and a few times I've woken up screaming. I tell Dad it's just a nightmare, and it is.

*

On Wednesday, I try and just blend in. I stand at the side and watch the girls dancing and laughing, and when they ask why I'm not joining in, I make a joke and say, "I don't want to show you all up!" (Which is sort of true because I am a pretty good dancer. One time in choir practice, Mrs Gallagher said, "James, the dance moves you're adding to the song are so … eye-catching! Maybe we could focus a bit more on the singing, though?" So, you see, it makes sense that I wouldn't want to show the girls up!)

Joel seems to realize that I'm not quite myself. At lunchtime on Thursday we wander around the playground, talking and laughing. Joel does most of the talking. He tells me about his favourite film (*Jurassic Park*, the original one), about his favourite food (pizza), and how he loves being outside. He tells me how he spends the weekends with his parents exploring, climbing, walking, discovering new places. He makes me feel safe, because Paul wouldn't dare say anything when Joel is around. Joel's just too cool, calm, chilled, too mature, too grounded for anyone to laugh at him or make fun of him. Everyone in the class seems to respect him.

And I can see why.

So, that's how my week passes.

Soon enough, it's my new favourite day, Friday – Poetry Day. This week Mr Hamilton asks us to write a poem about colour.

I write:

The Colours of My Life

Blue is spiders scuttling across a dusty floor.
Blue is a ghost's whisper drifting through
an empty house.
Blue is the cold moonlight slicing through the curtains.
It is a blanket of loneliness.

Red is a fire, crackling and burning softly.
Red is a laugh, a sneer and a cackle.
Red is the blood from my picked and ripped nails.
It is my anger, seething and writhing.

Yellow is a daffodil, nodding in the sun.
Yellow is a lemon, sour and bitter.
Yellow is music, floating on the breeze.
It is my hope drifting away.

OK, I know what you're going to say: it's very safe, very bland, very average.

Yes, I know! But I'm too scared to reveal anything more of myself – not right now, not when Paul might read it.

Mr Hamilton gives us time to illustrate and decorate our poems. Miss Clarke helps us too – she is *amazing* at art! Ameera's always talking to Miss Clarke, asking for tips and showing her the drawings she's done at home.

Joel is writing about the colour red, but he won't let me see his writing. He's deep in thought, chewing his lip with his tongue stuck out.

He looks silly, but not in a bad way, and I smile – for the first time in what seems like a long time.

"So, how was school, then?" Dad asks as we sit down to our Friday night dinner.

It's fish and chips tonight, which I hate, but I don't say anything.

He's been working long shifts this week and we've barely talked. He's been checking in on Nan, too, and helping her with her dinner – which is hilarious, really, considering his cooking skills. Nan says she usually throws whatever Dad makes into the bin once he's gone and makes herself something like bacon and eggs, or just a microwaveable meal. I do worry about her around the cooker with hot fat and oil spitting everywhere when she's so unsteady, but I'm sure she'll get better soon. I say that to her every time I see her – "I hope you get better soon" – and she smiles and pats my arm.

"School was OK," I mumble while pushing the greasy fish around my plate.

"Glad I asked," Dad replies sarcastically. "Am I going to get any more from you, or are you just too cool for school now?" He chuckles to himself.

Urgh, parents are embarrassing.

"It was fine!" I say. "Mr Hamilton had us writing poems again, which was great, and I've been hanging out with Joel at lunchtime. Did you know his favourite film is *Jurassic Park*?"

"Oh, Joel again," Dad says with a grimace.

I've done it again. Do not talk about Joel!

But then I feel myself getting angry.

"Why are you saying 'Oh, Joel again' like that?" I ask, scrunching up my face. I mean, he barely knows Joel.

But deep down I know why he's saying it. I'm *sure* I know what he's trying to say, what he really means underneath it all.

"You're just talking about Joel a lot at the moment,

that's all…" Dad says slowly through a mouthful of mushy chips and fish. "What's happened to Nathan and Harriet?"

"Nothing's *happened* to Nathan and Harriet. And I'm not *talking about Joel a lot*. He's just a new friend. He's kind, and he's brilliant at football … and maths … unlike me!"

"OK! OK! I was just asking about school!"

But he wasn't "just asking".

He thinks I'm gay. I know he does.

And he hates me for it.

So, I push him a bit further, daring him to say something, just waiting for a confrontation. "The choir are singing at Mr Hamilton's wedding as well, by the way, so that's exciting," I say, looking him dead in the eyes. "I'll need a lift and I've got a permission slip I need you to sign."

"We'll have a chat about that another time," Dad says lightly, and he gets up and begins clearing dishes away.

I feel another surge of anger.

Because we won't.

We won't talk about it another time.

CHAPTER 10

When I wake up, I have only one thought: *two days of nothing!*

Two days without Paul kicking the back of my heels and whispering my name.

Two days without that ache in my stomach and pain in my chest.

It's Saturday morning and Dad's been called into work. Again.

I'm on strict instructions to call if I need anything, but I'm in Year 6 now.

I can cope. *Chill out, Dad!*

I spend the morning relaxing in my pyjamas and listening to Mariah. It's a "Close My Eyes", "The Roof" and "Everything Fades Away" kind of morning. I sing along while having tea and toast. Dad tells me it's foul, but I *love* dipping my toast into milky tea until it's soggy. The important thing is that the toast has to be *covered* in butter. Nan's always done it, and so I've always done the same. It tastes so good!

Then I get dressed while dancing around my room to "It's Like That", "You Don't Know What to Do" and "Shake It Off", relieved not to have to close my bedroom door and hide my dancing from Dad.

When I'm ready, I video-call Nathan – thinking it's been aaages since we've properly hung out – but he doesn't pick up.

No worries! Next I video-call Harriet.

She answers, red and sweaty. "Heeeeeyyyy, James!" Her screen is shaky and I can hear Ellis, Harriet's little brother, in the background giggling and babbling.

"What are you doing?" I ask as Ellis makes a grab for Harriet's phone.

"Mum thought it would be a good idea to get Ellis some musical instruments," Harriet sighs over lots of banging and crashing and chiming. "And, *what a surprise*, I'm the one in charge while she does his snack and chats on her phone!"

"Hi, James, darling!" I hear Harriet's mum call from the kitchen. "Come round soon, OK?"

I can see now that Ellis has a maraca in one chubby hand and a small triangle in another. He's clanging them together, has food squished in his hair and is dribbling happily.

"James … you know how you're, like, my best friend? Well, what are you doing today?" Harriet asks sweetly, as she tries to hold Ellis still while he squeals with delight. "I mean, if you want to come and help look after Ellis I wouldn't mind!"

"Nnnnoooooooo way!" I laugh.

Babies are loud and messy and poopy, and I'm not sure why anyone would want one!

"Fine! You're a terrible friend!" Harriet says, but she's grinning so I hope she's joking. "Got to go now," she continues breathlessly, "but if you don't see me at school on Monday it's because I'm hiding down the garden from a loud, ANNOYING baby!"

"Oh, you WILL be at school on Monday," I hear Harriet's mum call out, then howl with laughter.

And with that she's gone. Harriet moans about Ellis quite a lot, but I know she's absolutely obsessed with him.

I wonder what it might be like to have a brother or sister? Would we play together and share secrets? Would we moan about Dad and roll our eyes at each other behind his back? Would we dance together to Mariah and visit Nan every day?

Actually, talking of Nan, I should ring her, or pop in and see her … but I decide that it can wait. I'll head to the library in town first, and then I can go and see Nan afterwards.

When I reach the library, it's cool and quiet and clean and calm. I like it here; I used to come down here with Mum when I was very little.

I smile and give a little wave to Mx Perry, the librarian, when I go in. Mx Perry has short silver hair, lightly tanned skin and I'm always surprised that they *don't* have a pair of glasses perched on the end of their nose like librarians do on TV. They've always got this excited, nervous energy about them, and they know everything there is to know about children's books:

You like scary books? I know just the one!

Want adventure? Romance? Graphic novels? Come this way!

Sci-fi and aliens? Have a try of this!

I wander up and down the aisles picking books up and putting them down again. I like reading; I like imagining all the different stories, picturing what it must be like to escape, to be someone else.

But I've also started feeling worried when I begin a new book. If Paul sees, will he tell me the book I chose is for girls? Judy Blume books, for example. My mum told me once that she used to like reading them when she was younger, so I suppose that's why I've started reading them now.

"Morning, James," Mx Perry whispers conspiratorially. I find myself flinching at the sound, in case they say "Jamesssss" like Paul does.

But that would be silly. Mx Perry wouldn't do that.

"I've got something for you," they carry on, and that's when I see they have something hidden behind their back. Intriguing!

"It's a book by Paula Danziger. I know you've read most of the Judy Blume ones, so this will be a good one to read next. It's called *This Place Has No Atmosphere*, and it's about a girl who has to go and live on the moon!"

They hand me the book and I whisper "thank you", floored by their thoughtfulness.

They nod and smile at me and then get back to work.

I clutch the book to my chest and head over to an empty desk. As I open the book and settle down, a soft, gentle pitter-patter of rain begins to fall. I pull my Mariah Carey hoodie up around my ears. It's black and says *I Don't Know Her.* I love reading when it rains. I feel all cosy and warm and safe.

I read for the whole of the morning, lost to the world, while rain trickles down from the dark sky. I'm enjoying my new book so much that I jump when my phone buzzes in my pocket. (Obviously, it's on vibrate – I'm in a library and I'm not a monster!)

It's Joel.

Where r u?

Underneath the desk, I text back:

Library 😊

He replies almost immediately.

Bored at home and stuck inside. Will come and meet u!

I smile to myself and continue reading, but every few minutes I look outside for Joel, waiting and hoping, filled with a strange excitement.

At last Joel arrives. His black, curly hair is stuck to his head. He's wearing walking boots, jeans and a waterproof coat. Very sensible.

I wave to him and he waves back and walks over. He takes off his wet coat and I see he's wearing a blue jumper underneath. It has a dinosaur doing a Rubik's Cube on it and says, *Clever Girl!*

I don't get it.

"Hi, mate!" Joel says. Except it sounds like the loudest bellow *ever*.

"Sssssshhhhh!" I say, giggling.

"Oh, sorry!" he continues in a very loud whisper that makes me laugh. "WHAT ARE YOU DOING? We could find out about Marsha P. Johnson, if you want?"

I gulp.

I suppose I can't put it off any longer.

My phone buzzes again, and I turn it off quickly without looking, hoping that I haven't disturbed anyone.

"That sounds like a good idea!" I say to Joel, although I'm worried about what else I might find out. But the library *does* seem the best place to carry out some research since I can't use Dad's laptop or my phone; I don't want him to find anything that might get me in trouble.

I say, "So all I know is that her name was Marsha P. Johnson and that she was something to do with the LG ... B..."

"LGBT," says Joel, smiling. "My mum says you

can't get rid of the 'T' because transgender people are an important part of the community."

I scowl. Why is it so difficult to say LGBT out loud in front of Joel? But he doesn't seem to mind, and we spend the next half an hour walking up and down the aisles, not really sure what we're looking for.

"What sort of books do you like reading, then?" Joel asks. We've found the history section, and we're just staring at the various titles of the books.

"Erm … well, I like Judy Blume books, and Mx Perry has just given me a book by Paula Danziger," I say, waiting for Joel to laugh at me.

But he doesn't.

"Cool! I saw you reading when I came in and wondered what it was."

He waits.

I look at the floor and then look up.

Why is he looking at me like that?

"So … go on! Tell me what it's about!" Joel says encouragingly.

"It's … well … it's about a girl called Aurora who thinks she's got her whole life sorted. She's, like, really popular and cool, and then her parents make her go and live on the moon with them, and she hates it and feels completely alone … and … that's where I'm up to…"

Joel seems to be really interested in what I'm saying. I start to feel embarrassed and realize I've been talking at him for ages.

"And what about you? What books do you like?" I ask.

"SSShhhhhhhhh!" comes a hiss from the other side of the library.

I shove my hand over my mouth, trying not to laugh.

"I like books about facts," Joel whispers, giggling. "Guides about the outdoors and identifying different creatures and birds and things."

"Oh, right, that's cool," I say, smiling at him. It feels strange to be talking to Joel about books like this. Strange, but nice.

Suddenly, Mx Perry pops up from behind a stack of books.

I nearly jump out of my skin! Where have they come from? How can librarians just sneak up like that?

"Need any help, boys?" they ask.

"We're trying to find out about an LGBTQ+ person from the past called Marsha P. Johnson," Joel replies, trying not to laugh at the sight of me jumping seven hundred metres in the air from shock.

"Perfect! Come this way," says Mx Perry, rubbing their hands together. "Sadly, we've only got one book about Pride and the Stonewall riots, but I can order some more in for you."

They locate the book, and we take it over to a corner of the library where there are beanbags. We slump down together. Because there's only this one book we have to share it, and I'm so close to Joel that our shoulders are almost touching.

I wonder what it would be like to touch his hand.

Don't be weird, James!

"Shall I read it out loud and you make notes?" he asks. "I'll do it very, very QUIETLY, though," he says, chuckling, "in case we get told off again!"

I nod and open my book of notes.

Joel smells of the outdoors – damp rain, grass and conifer needles.

Concentrate, James!

Joel begins and tells me that Marsha P. Johnson was a trans-rights activist and a really important person in the Stonewall riots in New York in 1969. He says that Marsha and her friend Sylvia Rivera fought for the rights and freedoms of the LGBTQ+

community. Marsha died in 1992, and it's unsure whether she was murdered or not, but some people believe the police never bothered to investigate it properly because of who she was: a Black, trans woman.

"Marsha P. Johnson sounds pretty inspiring," I say afterwards. "But what does the 'P.' stand for?"

"I skipped over that part, but apparently" – Joel giggles – "Marsha said it stood for 'Pay It No Mind', as in *mind your own business!*"

I laugh and we sit there for a while, flicking through the book and finding out about the Stonewall riots and other famous members of the LGBTQ+ community. As we read, I think about these amazing people and what a difficult time they had just for staying true to themselves.

I'm deep in thought, watching the rain, when Joel says, "It's horrible, isn't it, that people got treated like this just because they were different?"

He looks at me for a moment.

"I wouldn't care, personally," he adds, smiling timidly at me.

What's...? What's he...? Why is he...?

"Actually," Joel continues, "I've ... erm ... got something I want to tell you..."

My stomach starts to rumble and I start feeling hot, like I can't breathe quickly enough.

Why is he looking at me like that?

I think of Paul.

And I think of my dad, shaking his head in revulsion.

Gay.

Gay.

Gay.

"I've got to go!" I say, abruptly jumping up. I don't know what's going on or what Joel wants to tell me, but I just feel panicky, apprehensive, and my chest hurts. "I … forgot to leave a note for Dad, and he must be wondering where I am."

"OK, I'll walk with you," says Joel, getting up from his beanbag and stretching.

"No, it's OK! I need to go!"

And with that, I'm gone. I don't even put my book away. I leave Joel standing there, his brow crinkled.

Outside, the rain has nearly stopped; it's just a fine drizzle. I lean against the entrance wall and take a deep breath.

I hate this project. I HATE it! Everywhere I turn, everything I read, it's GAY GAY GAY GAY!

This project is going to be a disaster. As if Paul needs any more material to work with!

And what on earth is Joel up to? I begin walking home, a grim determination settling in my stomach. I'll push it all down. No more green eyes and holding hands. I'll play football this week, I will! Harriet can help me and show me. I can practise with her in her garden after school. Then Paul and everyone else will be impressed, and Paul will have no choice but to leave me alone.

It's sorted, it's all sorted. That's what I'll do.

Goodbye, Hello

Goodbye flick and swish and strut and twirl.
Hello throw and punch and shove and hurl.
Goodbye glide and shake and shimmy and dip.
Hello punt and boot and tackle and kick.
Goodbye whisper and giggle and a voice that soars.
Hello grunt and yell and growl and roar.
Goodbye sparkle and twinkle and glitter and shine.
Hello hide away, don't look up, stay in line.
Remove all traces, say goodbye.
Take a deep breath and live a lie.

*

The house is quiet and sombre when I get in. Dad must still be at work.

Dad! I turned my phone off in the library! I'm going to be in so much trouble! I fumble for my phone in my pocket and turn it on. There are fifteen missed calls, and then loads of text messages start to come through:

James, where are you?

Give me a call please!

James, I'm trying to get hold of you. Need to chat.

Please pick up phone.

And then my phone rings. It's Dad.

"Where the hell have you been?" he roars. "I've been trying to get you!"

"Sorry, I was at the library doing my school project," I reply, silently rolling my eyes. He's at work all the time. He's never here. Never. He can't just expect me to stay at home doing nothing all day!

"It's Nan…" Dad says. His voice is much quieter now, cracked and strained. "I'm so sorry, mate. It's Nan. One of her neighbours called. Her little heart … just…"

I feel dizzy.

I try to speak, but the words taste like acid.

My stomach twists.

My vision blurs.

"James, are you there? Nan's… She's died."

I feel everything slow and stop, and, like I've been punched in the stomach, I sink to the floor.

CHAPTER 11

That evening I feel like I'm in a daze.

A confused, angry daze.

We were at Nan's house all afternoon, and Auntie Kathy and Weird Bruce have just left. Weird Bruce patted me on the back and said, "Chin up, lad, chin up."

Dad has been making jokes and chatting to people on the phone loudly – "Oh, yes ... very sad... We're *fine*, though ... her time to go..." – and so it's not until nine p.m. when we sit down to eat. It's fish and chips *again*. I don't want it. I don't want to eat anything. I feel sick and Dad just *keeps* talking.

"I'll need to... Do you think we should...? I'll have to inform..." he's saying quickly.

He seems distracted, and his eyes are red.

Why is he talking so much when Nan has just died? It doesn't feel right, and it doesn't feel right to be eating, either, when she's not here. We should be sad and solemn and QUIET. Not *talking*. I push my cold chips around my plate and stare at the table while Dad continues babbling at me.

"And I'll… Well, James… I'll have to let your mum know, too…"

My head snaps up and I'm immediately filled with a scorching rage. I can't explain where it has come from.

"Mum? Why do you need to tell HER?" I spit the words out. They burn my throat.

"Because she's your mum and needs to be told," Dad replies evenly, but his voice has an edge to it, and I recognize the signs. The signs that say *do not push this any further*.

But it's too late. I'm furious and I want someone to blame and someone to shout at.

"She won't care! She LEFT, remember? *She left us*." I say each word slowly, but Dad shakes his head sadly.

"She *will* care. She's stayed in contact with your nan … all this time… She always visited your nan whenever she could."

What?! Didn't she leave us all to go and travel the world with her stupid fancy job?

"Why didn't I know this?" I ask, swallowing hard.

"You didn't want to know, did you?" Dad sighs. He seems tired and frayed. "Every time I mention your mum, you snap, or shut down. Every time she rings, you ignore your phone."

I stare at him for a moment, lost for words. So I should just forgive her? Pick up the phone and have a little chinwag and pretend that everything's OK?

No way.

I stare at Dad and feel sparks of anger crackling in the pit of my stomach. "I think I'm finished with dinner," I say firmly, getting up and pushing my chair away from me.

I pause at the door, readying my final words to him, knowing they will sting and hurt.

"I wish Nan was still here with me and you weren't."

I wait for Dad to shout and scream at me, for the argument I so desperately want, but he just shakes his head, and I walk out, leaving so much unsaid.

That night I can't sleep. I have a horrible headache and my eyes are itchy and tired. Everything aches and my throat is dry. And my feet – I just can't keep them still. They're tapping and jiggling away at the end of my bed. The room seems to be full of dark, menacing shadows stretching far and wide.

I want to go back. I want to rewind the day to before Nan died. Why can't I do that? It's not much to ask, is it? Just to go back and see my nan. To stop her from dying, or even just to say goodbye and tell her I love her.

It sounds bizarre, but I'm also *furious* at her for dying and leaving me here.

And why didn't she tell me about Mum visiting her?

Maybe if I hadn't gone to the library or been with Joel, I could have been there, and maybe I could have done something, and maybe everything would be different.

Is it because I thought about holding Joel's hand and his green eyes?

Doesn't God punish you for being gay? Isn't that what people say?

Is it because, deep down inside, I'm rotten? Because I must be a pretty awful person not to have told Dad about Nan's fall and chest pains. Maybe if I had told him, Dad would have put her in the care home, where they would have kept her healthy and safe. She could be there now if I hadn't been so selfish.

I wrap the duvet around me, but I'm shivering and my jaw is clenched and my teeth are grinding. I scream into my pillow and hit it again and again and again.

My Mariah Carey posters stare at me blankly.

Downstairs, I can hear Dad. He's sobbing quietly.

Eventually, as the darkness envelops me, I fall into a restless sleep.

CHAPTER 12

The next few days go by in a blur.

I stay in my room a lot, feeling sick and so, so tired. I sit in silence, the thought of playing any Mariah feeling disrespectful, wrong.

Nan is gone.

Nan is gone and it's my fault.

Dad, though, is full of purpose: *There's the funeral to organize! There's family to tell! So much to do!* When anyone asks, we both say *we're fine, we're fine, we're fine* ... but it doesn't feel like it.

Neither of us mention Mum again.

I stay off school. Harriet and Joel text me every day, but I don't reply. I wonder why Nathan hasn't called or sent a message. We used to spend so much time together in my room. He'd show me all his comics, and I'd play him Mariah, and we'd dance and laugh.

But it doesn't matter now; I wouldn't answer his texts or calls anyway. Harriet's mum drops off flowers, and I can hear Dad talking to her downstairs, but I don't leave my room. What's the point? Nan is gone. Nan is gone, and I don't know what to do.

So, I just sit in my room, staring out the window. At half past three every day I see kids walking past on their way back home from school, and it feels like a completely different world, one which I'm no longer part of.

On the first day I was off school, I saw Joel walk past at the end of the day. He caught my eye and waved up to me. But I ignored him, and since then I've always made sure I'm out of sight when I see him walking back home. Harriet tries video-calling me most days, but I don't pick up my phone.

What would I say to her?

Because I'm not quite sure what it is I'm supposed to do, or how I'm meant to act. I haven't cried yet. And I'm not going to. There's no point. Besides, I don't really *believe* she's gone.

I shouldn't say "gone". She hasn't gone anywhere – she's died.

For a few days, I thought that maybe Dad had got it wrong. I mean, he's not a doctor, is he? Maybe Nan had just been asleep and the neighbours thought she was dead and she'd been taken away. Maybe the ambulance workers had got it wrong too! I thought about Nan waking up in a cold, lonely mortuary and being stuck there. I wondered about finding out where they had her body, and going there, in case she woke up.

Because she might wake up for me.

Maybe I'm wrong, though? Maybe she wouldn't. Aren't I the boy who used to think that Mum would come home?

The days, hours, minutes, seconds pass by, and Nan doesn't miraculously appear. Dad veers from silent withdrawal to a manic happiness. He talks and talks and talks at the dinner table while I push the cold takeaway food around my plate.

Do I think we should invite some of her next-door neighbours? It's only a few weeks away, lots to organize! What songs should we choose for the funeral? Should we do a reading? Would you like to read something, James? Perhaps you could write a poem?

Could I write a poem, I wonder? What would I say? That it's all my fault?

But he looks at me so desperately, with such longing, that I can't say no.

Sure, I tell him. I can write a poem.

And even then, after I've said yes, he's still talking. Why is he talking so much? Isn't he sad? It just seems wrong to be talking or eating or laughing, because she's not here any more. I just want him to shut up, shut up, SHUT UP!

But on the days he does finally stop talking, he slips into a strange, trance-like state, and it's just as frightening. He sits at the kitchen table, with his newspaper open in front of him, and just stares at it. He looks exhausted and empty, devoid of any emotion. It's as if he has nothing left to give.

I understand how he feels.

Where does someone go when they die? I wonder. *Where are you, Nan?* I think about this a lot in my room, under my duvet. *Heaven? Nowhere?*

I don't know.

It seems so unfair to just be gone. To just vanish.

Guilt courses through me. Wherever she is, it's all my fault.

And I'll have to live with that for the rest of my life.

CHAPTER 13

"So then Ellis is crawling up the stairs NAKED with POO hanging out of his BUM, and Mum is SCREAMING and LAUGHING and it's SO GROSS! Babies are GROSS!"

We're round Harriet's house on Wednesday night, and it's the first time I've seen anyone or spoken to anyone since … you know. Dad's organized it with Harriet's mum. To be fair, I haven't left my room for days, just sitting in silence replaying everything in my mind. Everything I could have done and should have done.

Also, I haven't showered since Nan died, and, well, I'm beginning to smell a bit.

"It'll be good for you, son," Dad had said, and I realized that it would be easier to go than argue.

I don't think he knew that Harriet would invite Joel too. "Just … erm … maybe have a shower before you go," he had added, handing me a towel.

Harriet is currently regaling us with stories of her brother. "He's started saying 'doggy' and 'mummy' and 'oh no!'…" Like Dad, Harriet seems to be filling any awkward silences with as much noise as possible. But it's OK. I know she's doing her best.

We're in Harriet's room and it's covered in Marcus Rashford and Jack Grealish posters. (I know this because she's told me one hundred million times who they are. It's cool, it's like my Mariah posters, just without the fabulousness.)

I'm struggling to follow what Harriet's saying, but I smile at her story anyway. She looks over at me hopefully, and it's clear that she's desperate to make me laugh, as if that might take away all the pain. Then she coughs and looks around at Nathan and Joel. Her eyes are saying, *Help me out here, guys!*

But Nathan is on his phone and doesn't look like he wants to be here. I can understand that.

Harriet coughs again.

Have we run out of things to say already?

"And how's Sandra in Year 5, Nathan?" Joel pipes up eventually.

"How would I know how Sandra in Year 5 is?" Nathan grimaces, going redder and redder.

"Because you lloooovvve her?" Harriet cackles, punching Nathan on the arm again. She's smiling, but something doesn't seem right.

"No, I don't love her! We're just friends! Nothing else!" Nathan rubs his arm and looks completely mortified. I feel sorry for him.

He shakes his head haughtily and returns to his phone. I wonder who he's texting. Sandra in Year 5?

"And what about you, Joel?" Harriet asks. "Who do *you* fancy, eh?"

"No one!" Joel laughs nervously, but he looks at me quickly, and for some reason I feel a rush of panic. "We are in *primary* school, Harriet, and my mum says we shouldn't be worrying about girlfriends ... or boyfriends ... or any stuff like that at the moment!"

"Spoilsport!" says Harriet, crossing her arms. Then she glances quickly at Nathan and says, "For me, it's got to be Jack."

"Jack in Year 3?" Joel looks up, nearly spitting out his drink. "He's in Year 3, Harriet, that is GROSS!"

"No, not Jack in Year 3, you weirdo!" Harriet shoves him and laughs.

"Jack. Jack Grealish!" She drops to her knees in front of her Jack Grealish poster and starts blowing loud kisses up at it.

I roll my eyes and smile. Maybe Dad *was* right: I do feel a bit better. Although it's odd thinking that I'm sat here talking to my friends and laughing and eating crisps and listening to music (they're playing Mariah just for me) and Nan is gone—

Dead. She's dead.

And Mum keeps ringing and texting and wants to meet up, but I just can't. It's all hanging over me, like a shadow. I feel a pang of guilt and bite my bottom lip.

Harriet and Joel carry on, teasing and making fun of each other, while Nathan sits on the floor with his arms folded. At least he's put his phone down now!

I let my sadness wash over me, thankful that no one expects me to join in or laugh or talk about who I fancy at school.

Joel's right. It's primary school. And I can't start thinking about girlfriends ... or boyfriends. Not now.

No.

*

123

That night I dream of looking after Ellis, and he's babbling and giggling at first, and then soon he's saying "Jamesssssssssssssss, Jamesssssssssssss" again and again.

Suddenly Paul's there, joining in, and I'm surrounded by faceless people laughing and jeering and poking me. And in the distance, there's Mum. She's reaching out to me, and I'm trying to run to her, but I can't; I can't move.

I wake up, lashing out and screaming.

We Remember Everything

"Do you remember baking cakes,
clouds of flour and chaos everywhere?
The smell of crispy bacon on a Sunday morning,
laughing around the table?" the kitchen asks.
"What about the twinkling Christmas tree lights,
snow falling outside while wrapping paper
rustled?" the living room says.
"You used to love reading stories together.
You'd plait her hair while fairy tales
lulled you to sleep," sighs the bedroom.
"What a mess you made! Splish, splash, splosh!
Rubber ducks and water, water everywhere!

Humming while she washed your hair,"
giggles the bathroom.
"There was sunlight filtering through the trees,
BBQs, scuffed knees and lying on the grass
together," whispers the garden.
They all remember.
Dad remembers.
Dad remembers it all.
Me? I try to forget.

CHAPTER 14

Dad sits opposite me, shovelling cereal into his mouth and talking and slurping.

"It'll be good. Good for us to get back into a routine, won't it, eh, mate?"

I nod. It's Friday and the first day I'm meant to be back at school. My stomach rumbles and gurgles, and I can't eat breakfast. Yes, I want to escape the house and the oppressive air that hangs over us like a damp blanket, but I still don't think I can face school. I've argued and shouted, but Dad has made up his mind.

"Life goes on, son," he says brightly, but it's sad and forced, and I don't believe him. Not any more. "Besides, it's the weekend tomorrow, you can get through one day, mate," he continues.

I sit glaring at him for a while and then I ask lightly, "So, where's Mum now, then?"

She asked to meet me at the little café by the library, but I refused.

"She's staying at a hotel down the road while we pack up some of Nan's stuff. She's not here long, mate, because she's off again for work, but she says she'll be back again for the funeral in a few weeks."

I nod, my jaw set.

So, she's coming to the funeral.

I get up from the table, scraping the chair across the floor and leaving my soggy cereal sitting there in its bowl.

"James…" Dad hesitates. "Come on now. Clear away your bowl and spoon, please, mate."

"Do it yourself," I mutter under my breath, teeth clenched.

Dad sighs and runs his hands over head. "Fine. Fine. I'm not arguing with you today. Do you want a lift to school?" he asks.

"No," and then, just to annoy him, just to get a reaction, I say, "Joel's meeting me and we're walking together."

Dad takes a deep breath. "Fine. Have a good day."

I pick up my school bag and slam the door behind

me. My anger is like a tidal wave. I bite my lip and close my eyes to steady myself.

When I open them, I see Joel sitting on our front wall.

I feel the knot in my stomach untwist, just a little, and begin walking down the garden path.

Joel looks up from his phone as I approach and smiles at me. "Did you know that Mariah Carey has *nineteen* number one hits?" he says. "That's insane!"

"Of course I know!" I say, and I find myself smiling back. "But I appreciate the research."

It feels good to smile.

"And did you know that her father is Black African-American and Venezuelan, and her mother is White Irish?" continues Joel. "She says she never really felt like she fitted in when she was a kid. I can ... I can relate to that."

I nod, but I don't know what to say. I thought I was the only kid who felt like an outsider.

"Quick quiz, then," Joel says, and we start walking to school. "What was her first ever number one?"

"'Vision of Love'," I fire back without hesitating. "I can list them all in order, if you want?"

"No, no! You're all right!" he says, holding his

hands up in mock surrender. "And besides, I only know those three facts at the moment."

We walk in comfortable silence for a bit, then I say quietly, "Thanks."

"What for?"

"For not being weird about Nan and everything."

"That's all right, no worries. If you want to talk, we can."

"No, no, I don't think I do," I mumble.

We continue walking along, then eventually I say, "Now, shall we talk about Mariah's New Year's Eve debacle in 2020 and how she came back from the brink of disaster with wit, humour and courage and released one of her best albums to date?"

Joel bursts out laughing and says, "Go for it!"

"It's actually a good story for teaching people about resilience. Are you taking notes? Let's begin…"

CHAPTER 15

The first day back isn't too bad. When I walk into class, Harriet gives me a big hug and says, "I missed you."

"Thanks," I say. I find it hard to concentrate in lessons, though, and Mr Hamilton has to quietly remind me a few times what I'm supposed to be doing – but he doesn't make a big deal out of it. He doesn't even mind when I don't attempt to write during our poetry session.

Throughout the day Joel keeps turning round to check on me, and whisper to me, and make me smile.

Paul just glares at me, but I think he knows not to push it. Not today.

Nathan's being weird again and doesn't say hello

or ask me how I am or anything. In fact, it's almost like he doesn't know I'm there. When Mr Hamilton asks us to turn around and talk in groups of four, he refuses to look at me and only speaks to Harriet and Joel in short, clipped sentences.

Maybe he doesn't know what to say to me?

Sometimes people don't know what to say when someone dies and it gets awkward.

Maybe it's that.

At the end of the day, I say goodbye to Joel and Harriet. Nathan has already marched ahead and is nowhere in sight. I tell them I have some things to do, but really I'm just tired after school.

It's exhausting pretending that everything's OK.

I wander along, deep in thought, thinking about Dad and Nan and Mum and Nathan, and before I know it, I'm standing across the street from Nan's house. It's almost as if I've been in a trance, like I've walked here on autopilot, and it takes me a moment to realize where I am.

It's like a kick to the stomach.

I keep expecting Nan to pop her head out of the door or to hear music drifting out of the house, comforting and familiar all at once. Maybe, maybe she's just gone to Ruth and Eliana's house for a biscuit?

I push all the images and thoughts aside. Dreaming won't help.

"James?"

I look up, and as if I have conjured them, Eliana and Ruth are standing by Nan's gate. Spooky!

They look concerned, but their eyes are kind.

"Hi," I say. It's all I can manage.

Ruth sits down on the low wall along the pavement and Eliana stays standing, smiling uncomfortably at me. The cute-little-fluffy-rat-dog settles down at Ruth's feet.

"We are so sorry about your nan," she says.

Why does everyone say they're sorry, I wonder? Did *you* kill her, Ruth? No? Then what a pointless thing to say.

And then I think: *Well, maybe it is your fault. You promised to keep an eye on her and look after her and be there for her.*

But I know that's a horrible thing to think. That's all I seem to do at the moment, think horrible, angry thoughts.

"I imagine there's a lot happening now with planning the funeral," Eliana adds quietly. It's the first time she's spoken to me directly, and although she seems nervous about it, it's like she's making a real effort just for me.

"Were you the neighbours who saw her … you saw…?" I splutter, and I can feel myself starting to cry, but I stop immediately. I don't want to cry in front of them, in front of anyone.

If you cry, you're weak, and weak people get bullied.

Ruth stands up and puts a gentle arm around me. The cute-little-fluffy-rat-dog grumbles at the disturbance, does a little fart, and then lies back down again.

"Aw, James. We are so, so sorry," Ruth says again. Her voice is quiet. "We tried to help her, but she was already gone. I promise you, we did everything we could when we found her, and so did the ambulance crew."

I look at the ground.

Do not cry, James.

We stand for a while, looking across the street at Nan's house, saying nothing. The sky is changing from a peachy, golden amber to an inky, deep purple.

"You must have lots of brilliant memories of your

nan," Eliana says, and it feels like an invitation, a gentle invitation to remember and cry and laugh ... and let go. But I can't.

"Yes, lots. Lots," I say, picking up my school bag. "Anyway, erm, thanks for... I should get back home, or Dad will be worrying."

Ruth looks like she's about to say something, but Eliana looks at her and shakes her head.

Why do adults have all these hidden codes?

"Well, we're taking this little diva out for a walk, so we might as well walk your way," Ruth says. "Come on, madam." She gestures at the cute-little-fluffy-rat-dog.

"Do you want to walk her?" Eliana asks.

"OK," I say shyly, and then, "Mariah Carey has little dogs. She called one of them Jackson P. Mutley," I continue.

Ruth and Eliana laugh, and Ruth says, "Do you think Mariah goes out walking her dogs and picks up their poo?"

And I burst out laughing at the image that pops into my mind.

We walk the short distance home, and I tell them all about Mariah's dogs and their names, and it feels nice to share something, something of me, with people who listen and seem interested. Ruth and Eliana make sure I get to the front garden gate, and I wave and watch as they drag Miss Fluffy away (that seems like a good name for the dog, although I probably should find out her real name).

As I walk up the path to the front door, I start humming "Through the Rain" by Mariah. I feel a little bit like the old me is returning. I can make it through this, I'm sure I can.

But as I open the door and come into the house, I just know that something's wrong. Whenever anyone says that – "I just *knew* there was something wrong" – I think, *Really? Really, did you?* But there's something that puts me on edge.

That pain in my chest is back, and I can smell a burned stench coming from the kitchen. Dad is sat at the kitchen table with the kitchen light off, his head in his hands.

He looks up. His eyes are red and he looks … well, he looks furious. When he speaks, his voice is a choked whisper: "I cooked dinner for you, but you weren't here. *Again.*"

"Sorry," I say. "I … I went to Nan's house, and I got … I got upset, and Ruth and Eliana walked me home."

"*What?*" he nearly spits, his eyes flashing.

"They're Nan's neighbours, the ladies who live together a few doors down. The ones who found her…"

"I know who they are! What is it with you and … you and … people like *this*…?" he splutters.

"What do you mean?" I say slowly.

Go on, Dad. Go on.

Bring it on.

"Don't make me say it," Dad says darkly, and I wonder why he sounds like he's in so much pain.

"They were being kind to Nan and looking after her too," I reply finally. "I was upset and they walked me home."

"I don't want you seeing them again. They're … they're … *strangers*."

"But—" I begin.

"That's enough!" Dad snaps. "Go and get changed, and I'll do you some beans on toast."

"DON'T BOTHER!" I yell at him, and I slam the kitchen door and run upstairs.

What is it with me and people like "this"? People like "this"?

What he really means is, my son is gay and I can't stand to look at him.

Well, I hate him back. I promise now, in this

moment, that I won't speak to him *ever* again! He'll regret shouting at me and being horrible and he'll say sorry.

I put my Mariah music on and turn up the volume as loud as it will go. But for some reason it just makes me angrier today. I can feel my blood pulsing, and I'm grinding my teeth and squeezing my fists so tightly.

And then, suddenly, like a caged animal that's been let loose, I run at my bedroom wall and claw and slash one of my Mariah posters down. I roar and scream in agony and fury as I rip and shred the poster into tiny pieces until there's nothing left.

People like this?

People like this?!

Rip.

Shred.

Rip.

Tear.

Gay. Gay. Gay. Gay.

Afterwards, I sit amongst the torn fragments of the poster, my chest heaving, body shaking. I'm exhausted and curl into a ball.

Muddled

Everything seems so RONGW at the moment

Life turned USIEDP ONWD
Hopes and dreams MLDEUDD
Friendships BENROK
The word GAYGAYGAYGAYGAYGAYGAY
ringing in my ears

AGRNE bubbling and brewing and then overspilling
Can I UNALVER all this?

CHAPTER 16

"James, could I have a word for a moment, please?"

Mr Hamilton is smiling at me as he sits down. Miss Clarke is putting up a display for our "Famous Faces Throughout History" project. It's the start of a new week and we've been learning about the features of a biography and planning our presentations. Joel is so enthused and excited about it, but I can't summon up the energy to be bothered. It seems like one more thing to worry about.

After I'd cleared my torn poster away and hidden it deep in the bin outside, I spent the rest of the weekend hiding in my bedroom, stalking back and forth. Dad was out for most of the weekend, organizing Nan's house or weeding the garden or in the shed or going to the dump or ... basically doing anything he could to avoid speaking to me.

Suits me just fine.

But it's Monday now, a damp and drizzly day, and I suddenly realize that everyone has raced out to break, but I'm still sitting in the classroom, picking at my nails and staring into space.

"I just wanted to see how you are after ... after your nan?" Mr Hamilton says slowly. He looks a bit uneasy, and I wonder why adults always seem so nervous when they talk about these things.

"I'm fine," I lie. "It's good to be back at school." I give him a great big dazzling Mariah smile.

"Is there anything we can do for you? Do you want to pop over to the Sunshine Room and see Mrs Achebe for a chat at some point?"

I shake my head vigorously. *No, no I don't. Talking won't help. It won't bring Nan back.* "No, thank you, I'd just like to get back to normal and carry on." I force another smile, but a look of concern flickers across Mr Hamilton's face.

"I understand that," he says, nodding, "but, you know, if you need someone to talk to, or some time out at any point, just let me know. OK?"

"Cool! Yep, will do! Definitely!" I get up to leave, but I feel heavy and tired.

Mr Hamilton adds, "And is everything else OK? No other problems in class or anything?"

What is wrong with adults? I'm fine.

So, Paul has started following me around again and kicking the back of my feet. So, he calls me gay and says I have a voice like a girl. And Nathan and Jake and some of the other boys are being weird around me now too. It's hardly major or anything to get upset about.

Besides, I already tried to get a teacher to help, didn't I? I tried talking to Miss Wilson at the end of last year when it all started. I remember shuffling up to her and seeing her look of annoyance, like *I* was an issue, a problem, before I'd even opened my mouth.

"James, what is it?" she had said. "It's lunchtime and I have lessons to prepare, homework to mark, and it would be nice to actually eat some lunch for once."

I remember shifting my weight from foot to foot and just about managing to say, "Erm … well … Paul is calling me… Paul is saying I'm … *different*, and he keeps laughing at my voice."

I couldn't even say the word back then – I didn't want her to know what he said, in case she might think it was true – and I remember how I looked at the floor, so ashamed and so embarrassed to need someone's help, especially someone like Miss Wilson.

I remember how Miss Wilson was silent for a moment, her eyebrow raised. "And that's all?" she said eventually, and I remember the prickly heat rising up my neck. "There haven't been any physical attacks, any fighting or punching?"

I shook my head. "No ... but..."

"Can I suggest that you ignore it, then? Name-calling is such a silly thing to do. Paul's looking for a reaction, so don't give him one and he'll stop."

"But it's starting to happen quite a lot..." I said, feeling frustrated. My toes were curled in my school shoes.

"Well, thank you for bringing it to my attention, James. I'll keep an eye on it. Perhaps," she added, "you could start playing with more of the boys?"

I remember biting my tongue. I remember thinking, *So, it's my fault? It's my fault that I don't play football and that I like dancing with the girls and that Harriet is my best friend. I, what, deserve this?*

She was just like Dad.

I remember feeling like I wanted to punch her and scream at her, and how my stomach felt like there were waves crashing inside it.

But instead, I just mumbled, "OK … thank you."

I vowed never to talk to another adult about it again. So when Mr Hamilton asks if everything's OK, I can't bring myself to tell him. If I told him, wouldn't it be the same as admitting I'm … you know … *that word*? Mr Hamilton seems different, but I can't bear the thought of another teacher telling me not to worry and that I should act differently.

And if I tell Mr Hamilton what's going on, he might tell Dad.

Dad might tell Nan—

Not Nan, no. Not Nan any more.

Would Dad tell Mum, then?

No, I don't want anyone to know.

Maybe I could tell Joel?

No … he'd ask if … no.

So, I go for the safest answer: "Everything's fine, Mr Hamilton. I just haven't been sleeping that well since Nan … since Nan died, that's all."

Mr Hamilton looks like he wants to say something. He looks at me for a while.

I shift uncomfortably under his gaze.

"OK, James," he finally says. "Well, if you need any help or want to chat about anything – anything at all – you know where I am."

I nod and smile. I know.

But I won't ever speak to him about this.

CHAPTER 17

"Dad!" I shout up the stairs.

It's evening, and the first time I've spoken to him in the last few days. He's in the shower now, having come home after a long shift, and I'm going out.

I wait, kicking the bottom step over and over.

"What's up?" he finally calls down from the top of the stairs, a towel wrapped round his waist.

"Harriet's just texted. I'm going to hers to work on our school project." I make my voice sound flat and emotionless to let him know I'm *telling* him, not asking.

"Oh, right, OK… Bit late, isn't it? Does Harriet's mum know?"

"Yes, obviously," I snap. I'm not just going to turn up, am I? Obviously Harriet's mum knows. I think.

Dad nods. "And is anyone else going to be there?"

"Nathan, I think, because he's working with Harriet, and Joel because we're working together."

I wait.

I wait and watch his face try to settle on an expression.

Go on, say it. Say something.

"Oh, right. You're working with Joel on your project, are you?" His voice is sharp.

"Yes, Dad! I'm working with Joel!"

I can feel my face starting to flush and go red.

A frown flickers across his forehead and he says, "Fine, just this once. In future, it would be nice if you asked first and gave me a bit of warning."

I look up at him and narrow my eyes. "OK, well next time I'll predict when Harriet will invite me over, and you'll be the first to know," I say, and leave him standing at the top of the stairs looking defeated.

When I reach Harriet's house, her mum answers the door and scoops me up in an uncomfortable, tight cuddle – you know, the ones adults seem to love. But I like Harriet's mum. I mean, she's always wearing T-shirts with badly punctuated slogans on them and even has a "Live, Laugh, Love" sign in the kitchen, but I can forgive all that because she's always nice.

"Hello, darling James," she says. "How are you? How's your dad?" She's wearing a T-shirt that says, "This girls' 100% fabulous!"

I shudder.

"We're OK, thanks," I reply.

"And how are you feeling about the funeral next week?" she asks.

"Fine," I mutter, thinking of Nan's poem. I've still not written it.

"OK, well, they're upstairs. I just need to sort Ellis out for bed and then I'll bring some snacks and bits up for you soon, sweetheart, OK? You need to eat. I always say to Harriet, *that James*, he needs to eat. Especially after everything that's ... erm ... happened..."

I smile at her before heading upstairs because that always seems easiest when dealing with adults.

As I get near the top of the staircase, I can hear Harriet, Nathan and Joel talking in hushed voices.

"What do you mean, he's set up a WhatsApp group?" Harriet says, her voice a snarl.

"Exactly that! And he says if anyone talks to him then they're ... you know ... they're *it*, too," I hear Nathan reply.

Oh, juicy gossip! I rub my greedy little paws together in glee and feel a bit of that old carefree spark come back. But as I knock (Harriet insists on it) and enter the room, they all stop talking. They look guilty and Harriet jumps up straight away.

"JAMES! JAMES IS HERE!" she says excitedly, clapping her hands together and leaping about.

"What's going on? What's this about a WhatsApp group?" I ask, twiddling my fake moustache like that French – or is it Belgian? – detective Nan and I used to watch on TV.

Joel is silent. Nathan looks at the floor. I look at Harriet.

"Oh, nothing! It's a stupid WhatsApp group Paul's set up with some other boys in the class ... about ... football. Not me, though, I'm not in it!" Joel says. He looks at me reassuringly.

"Nor me!" Harriet says loudly.

As I look at the three of them, something doesn't feel right.

But maybe I'm just tired and being oversensitive? *Not everything is about you, James!*

It doesn't look like they're going to tell me any more, so I say slowly, "Ohhhh-kaaayyy, fine! Never mind, then! Forget I asked!"

"We should DEFINITELY start our research for this project, though!" Harriet says with a bit too much enthusiasm – or maybe she really is that interested in Emily Davison?

"I thought, maybe, you might do some sort of comic book for your presentation," I say quietly to Nathan, trying to bridge the seemingly insurmountable gap between us.

"No … nah… I'm over comic books and all that stuff now," he says dismissively, and it's like he can't look at me.

What is going on? Nathan loves comic books and superheroes! In reception we used to tie our school jumpers around our necks and use them as capes as we whizzed around the playground.

Inside Nathan's School Bag

1. Comic books and graphic novels. Miss Wilson told you they weren't "real books", but you never cared.
2. A sponge football. You once brought in a real football and smashed Harriet in the face with it. By accident. I think.
3. Your homework. You always do it straight away but hate handing it in, especially in front of Paul.

4. A notebook your mum and dad got you. You're designing and making your own comic book. You've only ever shown it to me. It's amazing.

5. A "Star of the Week" certificate from last year that you'll never show to anyone. "It's stupid," you say.

6. Your superhero trading cards and stickers. You know EVERYTHING about Spider-Man and Doctor Strange and Nightcrawler and Iron Man and…

7. The leftovers of your packed lunch. Always jam sandwiches with the crusts cut off. Your mum once gave you tuna sandwiches and it stank the classroom out, so you've only ever had jam sandwiches since.

8. A Mariah Carey key ring I gave you. We used to dance to her music in your room. You always said "Heartbreaker" was her best song.

9. A daisy chain from the first days of the summer holiday. We used all the fresh grass trimmings and twigs to make a bird's nest. We decorated it with daisy chains from my garden and you kept one. But I didn't see you much after that.

10. A note from Sandra. Maybe it says, "My darling, baby, gorgeous, hunky, super-cool, talented, tallest-boy-in-the-world Nathan: I LOVE YOU!"

But perhaps none of these things are in your school bag any more. Maybe there are other things in there. Maybe I don't know you at all.

"I was thinking," Harriet interrupts quickly, "we could do some sort of play about Emily Davison's life for our little presentation? And, Nathan, you could be the horse that killed her?"

"Might be in a bit of bad taste." Harriet's mum laughs as she waltzes into the room – without knocking, I might add. Harriet frowns at her mum momentarily, but her mum has a massive tray of sausage rolls and pitta bread and hummus and crisps, so all is quickly forgiven.

"Here we go, my little darlings!" she says with a flourish as she places the food on the carpet in front of us. She stands there smiling, and I bite my lip trying to suppress a giggle about how awks she is. I see that Joel is trying not to laugh too.

"So, what are you up to? What's going on?" she asks, clicking her fingers and doing some weird dance move.

"Muuuuuuuum, you're embarrassing me…" Harriet says through gritted teeth.

"Fine! I'll go! How's your dad, Nathan? And Joel, tell your mum we MUST meet up soon, and—"

"Muuuuuuummmm!"

"I'm going, I'm going!" She laughs as she backs out the door, trying to do a little dance shuffle thing and failing miserably. Harriet says her mum's set up her own TikTok account, which is clearly *mortifying*. No one over thirty should have a TikTok account.

Apparently, she's doing dances and all sorts on there, and Harriet is currently plotting ways to steal her mum's phone and hide it for ever.

"Urgh," Harriet says, shaking her head after her mum has left. "She's actually being SERIOUS, too! My mum is, like, honestly THE WORST!"

She looks at me and blushes. "Oh! Sorry, I didn't mean…" Harriet begins.

And then she looks at Joel and gasps and says, "And I didn't mean…"

"It's OK, it's OK!" Joel laughs as he grabs some crisps. He comes over and sits down next to me on the carpet, cross-legged. His knee touches mine, and he looks at me quickly, and then moves it away.

My heart starts to thud. But what if someone sees?

No one cares, James! Stop making a big deal out of everything!

In any case, Harriet and Nathan are now on the other side of her room, acting out the story of Emily Davison's life. Well, Harriet is. Nathan just looks miserable and is occasionally saying, "Neeiighhhh!"

Why the long face, Nathan?

"No one ever knows how to talk to me about my birth mum," Joel says quietly.

"Yeah, I get that. Everyone just usually avoids mentioning mine now," I say, picking at my shoelaces.

We sit in silence for a few moments, and then Joel says, "So, how's it all going?"

"I'm cool, we're cool. How are you?"

"I'm good," he says. I feel my heart thud again, and that excitement bubbling, but I push it back down. "I've listened to a few Mariah songs from her first album and—"

"Her first album is obviously a classic, but…" I say, waving my hand dramatically, "you want 'Daydream' and onwards. 'Butterfly' is when she broke up with her ex-husband and became all free and creative and stuff!"

"Noted," Joel says, doing an army-like salute. "So. Where were we with Marsha P. Johnson?"

"I've been thinking about that, actually," I begin. I feel like such a coward, but I continue and say, "I was wondering if we could swap with someone. Maybe do Maya Angelou or Ada Lovelace instead?"

Joel stares at me, confused, and his little nose wrinkles.

"It's just … it's just…"

But I can't find the words to say what I want to say. That I'm scared to talk about gay things because it will make people think I am gay.

"Come on, Marsha will be fun. Besides, you know that Mr Hamilton said no swapping! It'll be fine!" he says, patting my knee. He patted my knee. My knee!

Stop it, James!

"We've done so much work on it already, and she's such an amazing person," Joel continues. "Did you know that she worked with Sylvia Rivera to look after homeless LGBTQ+ kids? Can you imagine how much that meant to those kids?"

I didn't know that, and now I feel ashamed of myself. I'm being a coward, I know I am. He's right: it will all be fine.

"And I was talking to my mum about it," Joel carries on excitedly, "and she said there's so many people to celebrate in the LGBTQ+ community, who have contributed, like, to art and history and music. And she said, what about ending the presentation with some sort of acknowledgement of *all* their lives and achievements?"

"Sounds gay," mutters Nathan from across the room.

Harriet gasps, and we all freeze. The room goes silent.

I look at the floor and pray for someone to say something, anything.

Not Nathan too, please.

Harriet punches Nathan on his arm. She doesn't look like she's joking this time.

"Ow! That really hurt!" Nathan cries, backing away from her. It *would* look pretty funny, Nathan all tall and lanky recoiling in horror from tiny little Harriet, but none of us laugh.

"Is being gay a problem for you?" Joel asks, his voice icy. "Because Mr Hamilton's gay."

Nathan grimaces and shrugs and this seems to really annoy Joel.

"Maybe don't be such an uneducated, ignorant jerk," Joel hisses.

Silence.

Eventually Nathan mumbles something under his

breath and then reluctantly mutters, "Fine! Sorry."

Harriet and Nathan continue working on their project in silence, and every now and again I catch Harriet's face and she looks hurt and confused. She's moved further away from Nathan – she was practically sitting on his lap earlier – and now she's looking at him like she's trying to work out who he is and what happened to our sweet, kind Nathan.

I know the feeling.

"So, erm … what do you think?" Joel finally says, pointedly turning his back towards Nathan.

"That sounds like a really cool idea," I say. But everything has changed. Nathan has changed. Coming here was a mistake.

"Good! I'm glad you think that, because Mum has helped me print off *loads* of information, and I thought we could make posters or do like a PowerPoint or something about them … and…" He grins meaningfully at me. "I thought maybe we could play some Mariah Carey in the background at the end of the presentation? If you want. It's probably a cringe idea…"

"I LOVE it!" I say, all the awkwardness suddenly forgotten.

"OK," he says, pulling a stack of papers out of his

bag, "you take this pile, and I'll take this lot, and we can start reading about them all?"

I take the print-offs and look through them.

James Baldwin.

Barbara Gittings.

Freddie Mercury.

Keith Haring.

Jackie Shane...

Some of the names I've heard before, but there are *loads* that I don't know, and it feels odd that there are so many people who have done amazing, brave, inspiring things and I've never even heard of them until now! I spend the rest of the evening sitting next to Joel reading about these activists, artists, icons, influencers and pioneers and their lives, their dreams, hopes, ambitions, struggles and fights.

Why Can't I?

Why can't I sing like Freddie Mercury?
Why can't I samba like Johannes Radebe
and John Whaite?
Why can't I solve puzzles like Alan Turing?
Why can't I riot like Stormé DeLarverie?
Why can't I score goals like Justin Fashanu?

Why can't I paint two boys dreaming
like David Hockney?
Why can't I fight for the most vulnerable
like Sylvia Rivera?
Why can't I lead like Bayard Rustin?
Why can't I save lives like Alan L. Hart?
Why can't I just be myself?

CHAPTER 18

It's Tuesday lunchtime and I'm grabbing my packed lunch and heading outside into the playground. As I reach into my bag, I accidentally brush past Jake, who's also hanging around in the cloakroom. Perhaps he's avoiding going outside, too, and I wonder why that might be?

When I brush past him, Jake takes a deep breath in and seems to freeze.

"Oh, sorry, Jake, excuse me," I say. "You OK? Haven't spoken to you for ages. How are the stick insects?"

Jake looks terrified, his eyes wide. He blusters, mutters, shrugs and rushes out without even a backward glance.

What is going on?

As I walk outside, I see Paul. He's standing by the bench where I normally like to sit and read. Is he looking for me? Harriet and Ameera are at the other end of the playground, kicking a ball back and forth, preparing for today's BIG MATCH. I look at the ground and try and get to them, across the playground, without making eye contact with Paul or getting in his way.

"Everything all right, Jamessssssssss? *So* sorry to hear about your nan…" he says.

He doesn't look sorry.

Deep down, I'd been hoping Nan's death might mean he would start making fun of someone else. Does that sound horrible and selfish? Probably.

What I *want* to do is grab Paul and shake him and yell at him to never, ever mention my nan ever again.

But I don't. I just screw my face up at him like he's a piece of dirt and walk away, head held high, towards Harriet.

Almost there.

Keep looking up, James.

Almost there.

Harriet's so close, so close, if I can just reach her.

Suddenly Paul's standing in front of me, snarling. I can see his teeth and smell the strong odour of his

Lynx Africa. (It's actually pretty repugnant.)

Paul's taller than me and I have to crane my neck to look up at him.

"What do you want, Paul?" I ask, but already I can feel my bravado slip away.

"You think you're so much better than everyone," Paul hisses. "Always prancing around in the playground with your stupid gayboy dances!"

Paul is looming over me now.

I think, *This is it, he's going to hit me. Come on, James. Come on! Do something. Anything.*

But instead, I flinch and back away from him.

Paul takes another step forward. "You're just a stupid gay with a stupid, gay, girl's VOICE!" he shouts in my face.

I feel my whole body freeze in fear. I should hit him. *Do something, James!* I curl my fists up but my breathing is jagged, short. I can't do this... I just can't hit someone.

Suddenly we hear:

"Oi!"

It's Harriet. She races over from across the playground, a warrior. She shoves Paul away from me. It's a hard shove, and Harriet looks enraged. She squares right up to Paul. She's smaller than him, but he looks worried, like he doesn't know what to do next.

"Leave him alone!" she screams in his face.

Harriet really is quite frightening. She is now centimetres – millimetres – away from Paul's face. I see anger crackle and sparkle in her brown eyes. And then when she speaks again, her voice has turned to a low, threatening growl: "Don't you *ever*, ever, go near my best friend again."

It's as if time has stopped. Some of the other children have realized that something's going on, and I can see Joel running across the playground, looking concerned.

Harriet jabs at Paul's chest. "I *said*" – she jabs him again – "don't EVER go near him again. Got it?"

Paul looks furious, but as Joel comes over and Ameera steps forward, he also realizes he's outnumbered. "Yeah, whatever, Harriet! I was just mucking about, you loser!" He pushes past her and stalks off towards the water fountain, where Jake and Rafe are kicking a ball.

Nathan is there too, just standing there, watching with his mouth open.

I see Harriet breathe a sigh of relief. She turns to me. "James, are you...?"

I can't look her in the face – I'm too upset, too

embarrassed. "Why did you do that? It was just Paul being Paul…" I mumble in reply.

"I was trying to help. We need to talk about this, James." She steps towards me, but I back away.

"Yeah, yeah, we will. I just need…" I turn and start walking.

What do I need? I don't know.

I feel ashamed. Is that weird? Ashamed that I needed Harriet to come and save me. That I didn't have the courage to stand up to Paul.

I think about Nan, and how she was so full of life, and how she'd be so disappointed that I just let him … let him speak to me and treat me like that.

"James, please, what's going on?" Harriet begs, trailing behind me.

"Just LEAVE me alone!" I finally snap, rounding on her. "You always do this! You just rush in and don't think and you've made EVERYTHING worse!"

Harriet looks like I've slapped her in the face.

She goes to say something, but I interrupt and say, "I need to get to choir," and then I turn and walk away, feeling horrible.

And it's then that I realize that school has changed for me. It's a scary, lonely place, and I don't feel safe here any more.

I spend the start of our extra choir practice sitting in the boys' toilet. Oh, the degradation! They smell of wee, and they're damp and grotty and gross. I sit in a cubicle with my feet lifted off the ground because I think a kid in reception has tried to use the toilet and ... well, *missed*, and the floor is soaked. It's grim and my new school shoes are pretty fabulous (black brogues with buckles, if you must know) and you have to have *some* standards, even if you are a social outcast.

I'm so annoyed with myself! I think of all those people Joel and I read about who fought for their rights and fought to be heard and seen. Like Nancy Cárdenas, who came out on television, and Bayard Rustin, a gay man who fought alongside Martin Luther King Jr. for Black Americans' rights. And here I am sitting in the toilets feeling sorry for myself.

And this is nothing, *nothing* like what some people face every day. It's just one horrible loser making my life miserable. Boo hoo me. Very sad.

I punch the cubicle wall.

I hate how angry I am all the time now, and I hate missing choir and I hate not being able to dance and sing and perform in the playground. It's like there's no more sparkle, no more glitter left in the world, anywhere.

What a waste of space I am, hiding away in a rank, smelly toilet cubicle. What a cliché! Can you *imagine* if anyone found out? I'm meant to be enjoying Year 6, having fun and being carefree, but this? This is rubbish.

All because Paul says I'm *that word*.

And I can't tell anyone, not even my friends, because it would be like admitting to feelings that I don't really understand or know about yet. Anyway, I'm a kid. I'm eleven. I don't know if I am *you know*, and I don't want to decide yet. Deciding seems so final. Why are adults always trying to decide which box or category we all fit in? What's wrong with not knowing or not wanting to decide just yet?

But maybe it would be good to decide, just to confirm what I feel, to have a name for those feelings? Maybe I'd feel less alone? Free? Like I was part of something?

You have to keep going, have to be strong. Mariah always says that, doesn't she?

And what about Mr Hamilton painting his nails and getting married, and Eliana and Ruth, holding hands, and Marsha P. Johnson?

Pay it no mind.

You have to get on, so I get on.

I wipe my eyes, open the toilet door slowly, and check that Paul isn't waiting for me.

He's not there, and I breathe a small sigh of relief. I splash some ice-cold water over my face and look at myself in the grubby mirror.

What would Mariah Carey do? Come on, James! What would she do?

She'd defy anyone who second-guessed her. She'd sing her heart out while she looked them all straight in the eye.

You can do this, I say to myself.

And I can. I can do this.

Shoulders back. Sort the hair out.

Gorgeous!

Off to choir. I'm going to choir.

CHAPTER 19

"Where have you been?" whispers Joel, looking annoyed and worried.

I sidle in next to him, and Mrs Gallagher is so busy conducting the choir that I don't think she's even noticed me creep, mouse-like and stealthy, into the room.

I say to Joel, "I just didn't feel well, that was all. I'm fine now, though!" I give him a great big show-biz Mariah beam and hope it fools him.

It doesn't.

"What was going on with Paul and Harriet in the playground?"

"Nothing, honestly, just drop it."

"No. What was going on?"

"NOTHING!" I yell, much louder than I meant to, even surprising myself.

And just then, like in one of those dreadful comedy shows that Dad watches, everyone turns and stares at us. Mrs Gallagher pauses the music and folds her arms.

"Boys, is everything OK?"

"Fine," I say with a wide smile. Everything is fine.

"Well, perhaps we can get on with the song, then? We don't have long to rehearse for Mr Hamilton's wedding!"

The music continues, but I can't bring myself to speak, let alone sing. Joel looks furious next to me, and dejected and miserable too. And of course, I feel bad. It seems like all I do lately is push away the people I care about.

At the end of the practice, Mrs Gallagher gathers us around for a chat. She's wearing blue leggings today with a white dress over the top. It's got a coffee stain on it, and she has three pencils protruding from her bun.

"Now, I NEED, NEED, NEED," she says with a clap for each word, "those permission slips back by next choir practice, OK? You've had AGES for your parents to sign them!"

The permission slip! I start to fidget uneasily and look out of the classroom window at the children in the playground whizzing by. Could this day get any worse? I feel sick at the thought of asking Dad.

"I KNOW the wedding's a few weeks away," Mrs Gallagher is continuing, "but I NEED to know who's coming on the Saturday, and how you're getting there and so on. James, are you listening?"

"Yep, yeah… I mean, yes, Mrs Gallagher."

Mrs Gallagher rolls her eyes and shakes her head theatrically.

"So, everyone," she says, "make sure your adults sign these and get them back to me! Great rehearsal today – despite the interruptions."

She looks pointedly at me and Joel.

"Right, off you go, well done, EVERYBODY!"

I spend the rest of the afternoon desperately trying to concentrate on Mr Hamilton and our science lesson.

Harriet is refusing to speak to me. And I'm so ashamed at how I spoke to Joel in choir, I can't even look him in the eye.

And the permission slip! I can't keep just ignoring it and hoping it will magically be signed, can I?

I drag my thoughts back to our science lesson. This half of the term we're going to be finding out about blood and circulation and nutrients and exercise.

I've been looking forward to this topic for *ages* because last year the Year 6 kids told us as part of it they got to dissect a *real* heart!

When I first heard that, I wondered if Mr Hamilton was a serial killer. In fact, Ishir in the year above told us it was the hearts of children who misbehaved, but it turns out it's actually an animal's heart you dissect. (Which is still pretty cool.)

Anyway, when Mr Hamilton tells us that we're going to be setting up an experiment in groups of four with the table in front, I look at Harriet, Joel and Nathan and groan inwardly. What a day!

It's very difficult working in a group where no one seems to be talking to each other. Why isn't Nathan talking to me, and why does Harriet always seem to be glaring at him now? What is going on with us all?

Mr Hamilton keeps coming over to see if we're OK and asking who's making notes and so on, and he gets lots of mumbles and mutters and grunts from us, like we're *teenagers* or something.

Today, it turns out that we aren't cutting open hearts just yet; we're measuring how exercise affects our heart rate. We have to record our resting heart rate and then run around the playground, and then take it again, and *then* we have to share the results and plot them on a graph, and *then* we have to make a conclusion. They really do work us hard in Year 6!

Paul and Jake and Ameera and Rafe are laughing and cheering each other on as they take it in turns to run around the playground. But Harriet refuses to take Nathan's pulse, and Nathan seems to recoil when I ask him to take mine. And then Joel gets really cross at having to take Nathan's pulse, and Harriet refuses to run round the playground, and it's all just a big, confusing, *horrible* mess.

Near the end of the lesson, we basically – and *don't* judge me – make up our results. It's all we can do. Something is bubbling and brewing beneath our silence.

None of us speak for the rest of the day. I even find it difficult to follow along during story time. Mr Hamilton *always* makes time for stories, saying it's the most important part of the school day, and I usually love story time, just sitting and letting the words wash over me and dreaming and imagining that I'm there *in the book*.

But today, I can't focus, and I keep looking across the classroom to see if Paul is still looking at me, but every time I do he's facing forward. A couple of times

I catch Jake's eye, but he just turns away and pretends to be listening intently to Mr Hamilton.

And before I know it, we are stood behind our tables getting ready to leave, and it's *so* close to all being over. We are so close to home time. Nearly there.

But then Mr Hamilton says, "No one is going anywhere, 6H, while we still have three school jumpers on the cloakroom floor. Do they have names on them, Miss Clarke?"

"I'm afraid not, Mr Hamilton. You really need to make sure you put your names on these, please, Year 6," Miss Clarke is saying while inspecting the labels. She's wearing purple dungarees today with hearts and rainbows printed on them.

"Let me have a look!" says Ameera, and then Rafe says, "I'll help too!"

They take the jumpers from Miss Clarke, who looks slightly bemused. Then they hold one out and each takes a deep, deep sniff of the jumper.

"This one's Summer's jumper," says Ameera confidently, and Rafe nods his head and says, "Yep! Definitely!"

Summer jumps up and takes the jumper from Ameera, looking grateful.

"And this one" – Rafe takes another deep inhalation and sniffs the jumper, which has bean stains and mud on it – "this one belongs to Harry."

Mr Hamilton is standing at the front of the class, shaking his head and laughing.

"And this one…" Ameera pauses and looks at Rafe. "Need some help here!" She giggles.

They hand the jumper back and forth, and by now we are all in stitches (even me) and Miss Clarke seems both horrified *and* impressed.

"We *think* this is Anna's jumper," Ameera finally says triumphantly after a long, intense sniff of it.

Anna skips up to Ameera and Rafe and sniffs the jumper. "Oh yes, it *is* mine," she says, laughing.

"Well, I think we'd better give our resident jumper sniffers a round of applause, don't you?" Mr Hamilton says, and we all start clapping and cheering, and Ameera and Rafe take a bow.

As we leave, it almost feels like everything is back to normal. I could just pretend, couldn't I? That everything is fun and that we are a class again, a team who have one another's backs.

But Harriet stomps off in front of me, and Nathan runs to catch up with Paul and Jake, and Joel is hanging around at the back of the line, deep in conversation with Summer and Ameera. I hope they'll forgive me and just forget about today.

So, I walk home on my own and I feel like a dark storm cloud is gathering over my head. I feel like someone, *something* is following me, and I keep stopping and checking, making sure that it isn't Paul.

I stop by Nan's house on the way back and stand there. The sky is grey, and I keep waiting for her to shuffle out of the door and to hear her music, lilting and soothing and full of life.

But the door stays shut and no one comes.

Nan's House

The house kept you safe and
Wrapped you in all your favourite smells:
Granddad's aftershave.
Perfumed talcum powder.
Sweets and chocolate biscuits.
Fragrant freshly cut grass.
Scent of lavender and bluebells
drifting in on the breeze.
Your newborn grandson.
The smells of happiness and a life well-lived.
The smells of home.

CHAPTER 20

When I get home, the house is quiet again.

Dad is working and then going to Nan's to sort out her bedroom and living-room furniture. We're giving some of it to a charity, and it feels strange to think that other people will be sitting on Nan's special chair.

I wonder what Mum is doing now. Is she at Nan's, helping Dad?

I make a snack (crisp sandwich, very nice, thank you very much) and spend some time doing my homework.

But I can't concentrate: *Paul, Harriet, Joel, Nathan, Paul, Harriet, Joel, Nathan. Paul, Harriet, Joel, Joel's face in choir, choir ... wedding... Permission slip!*

I think about it sitting in my bag. Is there any

point, I wonder? Should I bother asking Dad? I know he's just going to say no. He says no to everything.

I spend some time practising forging Dad's signature. I have a notebook full of pages where I used to practise my own signature all the time because obviously as a famous songwriter writing for Mariah I'd be doing autographs for fans. But trying to recreate someone else's signature is hard! Dad's signature is just a scribble and a scrawl, and I get more frustrated the more I try to perfect it.

Maybe I could ask Mum? She *supposedly* wants to be back in my life now, and it's the least she can do.

But the thought of asking her, of speaking to her, of needing something from her, makes me feel sick.

So, I sit, and I sit.

Finally, I "address the elephant in the room", as Nan would say.

If she were here.

I can't put it off any longer.

I have to get Nan's poem written for the funeral. But I can't think of what to say about her. How do you summarize someone's life in a few lines? I think about how I could celebrate Nan's life and remember her and do her justice.

But all I write is:

I once had a nan
And she liked cheese and ham

Not only is it a pretty awful start to a poem, it's also not true. Nan would *never* eat ham and cheese in a sandwich, *not together, James!*

Everything seems stuck in my mind now, whizzing and spinning around again and again.

I spend the rest of the afternoon in my bedroom listening to Mariah. It's a "Looking In", "Twister", "Sunflowers for Alfred Roy" kind of day. Sad ballads for a sad boy. I begin to torture myself wondering what Harriet and Joel and Nathan are up to. Probably hanging out together now at the park, or something like that, relieved that I'm not around. Everything back to normal and sorted between them without me there. They're probably all talking about what a terrible friend I've been recently.

And it's true. I've been pretty awful: I've been snappy and cranky, and I don't think I've even asked how they're doing or what's going on in *their* lives, not once.

It's just been me, me, me, and I can't have been much fun to be around. Everything that's happened recently has been my fault – Nan dying, and Paul being horrible, and my friends being cross with me, and Dad being sad about Mum and hating me.

And in amongst it all there's Joel.

Before I know it, hours have passed by and my room is getting dark, and I've got no further with the poem for Nan.

I did write this, though:

Writer's Block? Search Here for Inspiration!

5 tips for eliminating writer's block.
Clever poem about writer's block.
Moving poems about death.
Inspiring poems about grandmas.
Coping with grief and loss.
3 ways to forge a signature.
Tips to effectively ask for help.
Bullying definition and meaning.
How to tell if you like someone.
Am I gay? 6 questions to ask yourself!

Then I hear Dad come in, and so I slowly head downstairs, my heart in my mouth and thumping hard because I know I need to show him the permission slip and ask if I can go.

When I walk into the kitchen, Dad has his head in the fridge and looks guilty.

"Are you DRINKING from the milk carton?" I yelp, astonished.

He shakes his head, but he can't speak because his mouth is clearly *full* of milk! He gulps it down and laughs. I haven't heard him laugh in a long time.

"Definitely not!" he says, shaking his head again.

"Because, you know, you tell *me* I can't drink from the milk carton and have to use a glass?" I try to raise my eyebrow in exactly the now-listen-here way he does.

"And that's exactly what you have to do, son. Don't do as I do, do as I say!" he says, wagging his finger at me in a really overexaggerated way like I'm a little kid again. It makes me chuckle and roll my eyes.

But I'm not *really* cross at him for once, and it seems to have broken the ice between us. We used to laugh a lot, before Mum left and Nan died. Now he just seems beaten down by everything, so fed up and tense and tired.

But today it's nice to see him like the old Dad he used to be.

"How's your poem coming along for Nan?" he asks, sitting down at the kitchen table.

"Erm … it's getting there," I lie. "Um, I've got something to ask and I *know* you're going to say no…"

"Well, why don't you try me and see?" answers Dad brightly, and my heart lifts. Maybe he *won't* say no?

"The choir is going to be singing at Mr Hamilton's wedding…" I can see Dad's face cloud over, and he stands up and begins to move around the kitchen, putting things away and clanging pots and pans loudly.

"We've got a permission slip that needs signing for us to go. It's the weekend after Nan's funeral, so I won't miss any school, and we've been rehearsing all term and…"

I trail off because Dad doesn't seem to be listening.

"Dad?" I ask.

"Yes, yes, I heard you. I … erm … don't see why this teacher of yours needs kids singing at his wedding, son…"

"Well, that's the cool thing … it's a *surprise!*" I say.

"I don't think it's appropriate, mate, to be at a teacher's wedding. Sorry. Now, what do you want for dinner?"

I can feel tears stinging at my eyes and a volcano of pain and fury bubbling in my stomach.

"But WHY not? I want to go!" I say.

I know why not.

Go on. Just say it, Dad.

JUST SAY IT!

"You're behaving like a baby, James. I've been working ALL DAY and then I've been at Nan's place and trying to make calls to do all the funeral arrangements, and now I come home to this! Just leave it. You're not going."

"You'd let me go if Mr Hamilton was getting married to a WOMAN!" I shout, fists clenched.

And it's there, it's finally out there; I've said it and I can't take it back.

Dad freezes, his back to me. He is like a stone statue, and an oppressive silence hangs in the air.

"You're. Not. Going," he finally says quietly, punctuating every word slowly.

He seems broken, and hurt, but I don't care any more.

"I hate you," I whisper. "And Nan would too."

I turn around and leave the kitchen. It feels like we won't ever be able to come back from this.

CHAPTER 21

The following morning, I wake up feeling groggy. My head feels heavy. I've hardly slept. The light from Dad's room seeped under my door and kept me awake, and I know he was up all night. I could hear him pacing and shuffling, and a few times I thought I heard him crying. And I feel terrible, absolutely awful, that it's because of me. Guilt grabs me round the throat and makes my chest feel tight.

At breakfast, Dad won't look at me, and leaves for work without saying a word. Not one word. No reminder about homework, no making sure I've eaten breakfast or have my PE kit or anything like that.

I thought I'd feel angrier about it all, but I just feel empty now. Empty and useless and tired.

*

I walk to school on my own, barely looking where I'm going and hardly registering how I get there. I wait outside the school gates alone.

It's only Wednesday, so I prepare myself for the days ahead.

<u>Instructions on How to Make It Through</u>
First, act like everything is fine with Harriet
and Joel like yesterday never happened.
Be as small and quiet as possible. Do not draw
attention to yourself by putting your hand up.
Your voice is girly; don't let anyone hear it.
Next, it is important to try and remain invisible
in the playground. Don't sing or show off.
Don't smile or laugh. Tell Harriet you're not
feeling well. Tell Joel you're just tired.
When lining up after break, keep your head down
and look at the floor. If you hear any whispers of
gay, poof, sissy, girl, gayboy, just ignore them.
When friends ask if anything is wrong, smile
and tell them that everything is fine.
During choir rehearsal, keep your dancing
and swaying to a minimum.
At lunchtime, smile and laugh while Joel,
Harriet and Ameera chat.

Try and force down your food,
even though you feel sick.
In addition to this, it is important to note that
time spent with Joel should be limited. Lunch is
fine, but no one wants to see two boys giggling and
whispering in the playground. Especially not Paul.
Instead, ask Harriet if she'll kick a ball around with
you. You do need to get better at football, after all!
Keep checking over your shoulder. Paul might be there.
In assembly, ignore it when he whispers
"Jammeessssss" or kicks the back of your
feet when you leave the hall.
Make sure you hand your homework in on time
and behave impeccably. If you get in trouble,
your dad might be called into school
and then it will all come out.
After school, tell Joel and Harriet you've got
loads of homework and that your dad is making
you help at your nan's. You can't hang out
with them as much as you'd love to.
At dinner, sit in silence. It's for the best.
Anything you say will make it worse.
Ignore any attempts Dad makes to talk to you.
Ignore the fact that he looks gaunt and haunted.
Forget your nan.

To succeed, you should keep music to a minimum.
You don't deserve to listen to Mariah Carey
anyway, you big gay. No "There Goes My Heart". No
"Slipping Away". No "There for Me". NO MARIAH!
At night, collapse into bed. You will be tired from all
this pretending, all this hiding, but isn't it worth it?
Follow these instructions and you will make it
through the week. Tired, afraid, desperate,
yes, but you will make it through.

I follow these steps, and Friday finally comes around. Even the thought of poetry can't make me feel better, because the only poem that matters, Nan's poem, won't come.

So, Friday is just another day.

And it's about to begin.

I drag myself through the first lesson, and at break time I sit alone.

Harriet asks if I want to kick a ball around with her again today, but I say *no, thank you*. I've kept everything light and breezy between us. I haven't mentioned her pushing Paul, and I just hope she's forgotten about it.

Joel asks if he can sit next to me and read his

book. He's got a Judy Blume one out of the library. But I say, *No, thank you. I'd like to be on my own so I can think about Nan's poem. Our poetry session is after break this week and I need all the time I can get if I'm going to get this done.*

But I can't concentrate, and I keep rereading what I've written over and over again.

I keep rereading what I've written over and over again.

I keep rereading what I've written over and over again.

(Sorry ... couldn't resist! I'm even funny when my life is in tatters.)

I notice Sandra and Nathan wandering around the playground perimeter (oh, hello, maths!), laughing and whispering, their heads so close to one another.

I hope neither of them has nits.

I think of when Joel kept me company in the playground after Nan first died. I think of how we talked and laughed and whispered then, just like Nathan and Sandra now.

But I need to protect Joel. People might start talking about him next.

After break, we line up outside the classroom for Mr Hamilton, and Paul stands behind me kicking the back of my feet, ever so lightly, just to let me know that he's there.

He whispers, "Jamessssss, Jamessss. Where's your little friend Harriet? Jamesssssss. Jamesssssss, you big gayboy..." over and over again and his sidekick, Jake, laughs too.

Harriet's meant to be lined up next to me, but this time she's at the front of the line talking to Ameera. She keeps laughing really loudly and then looking over at Nathan, who's busy talking to Rafe and doesn't seem interested at all.

Paul keeps kicking my heels, and I feel my skin prickle and acid rise in my throat. It is so infuriating that another kid can do this to me. My heart starts beating faster and faster and I'm sure the veins in my forehead must be close to bursting.

"Jammmmeessss. Jammmmesssssss. Not prancing around the playground today, then?" This time it's Jake.

"Oh, be careful, Jake!" Paul says. "He might kiss you if you get too close!"

And then something in me finally snaps.

I turn around and blurt out, "Leave me alone!" I realize as soon as I say it how pathetic I sound. I can't look them in the eye.

Paul and Jake just burst out laughing in my face, and I feel ridiculous.

"Oh my god! Did you hear his voice?" cries Paul. "So gay!"

And then Paul and Jake immediately stop because Mr Hamilton's rushing along the corridor with Miss Clarke beside him.

"Well done, Paul and Jake, great to see two of our class are in pairs and ready to go in!" Mr Hamilton says. "Harriet, where should you be?"

We file into class and I say nothing to Harriet as I sit down.

"What *is* going on with you?" she whispers. "Is it Paul still? Do you need me to have a word? Or beat him up?"

She goes to stand up and I pull her back down quickly.

"I'm fine," I whisper. "Stop going on about it."

"I'm just trying to help…" Harriet spits back, but luckily I'm saved from any more questions because it's time, finally, for poetry.

Mr Hamilton tells us that today's poetry theme is all about memories, and we listen to a poem called "Childhood Tracks" by James Berry.

We're meant to spend some time in groups of four talking about the poem. Joel is the only one who offers any ideas in our group. Nathan is making funny faces across the room with Paul and Jake, and Harriet is sitting next to me, slumped in her chair, with her arms folded.

We read some other poems linked to memories, and then Mr Hamilton invites us to try writing our own poems.

Of course, for me that means Nan's poem, for the funeral.

I have to do it. I can't put this off any more.

So even though all I can think about is Paul and Jake and what they might say next and if I've upset Harriet again, I take a deep breath.

It's now or never.

After a few minutes, I start thinking it's never.

I *want* to write the poem, but the words still won't come. I sit chewing my pencil and looking out of the window. Everyone else around me is writing now, but it's like my mind is full of swirling fog and I can't concentrate. What kind of poet – what kind of *grandson* – am I if I can't find the words to celebrate Nan's life, or say goodbye?

"James, how are you getting on?"

It's Mr Hamilton and he's kneeling down next to my desk, so I have to look at him.

I shrug. I consider saying something sarcastic like, "Oh yeah, GGRREEAATT! Couldn't be better!", but Mr Hamilton hasn't done anything wrong and maybe I do need some help.

"I … I'm trying to write a poem about my nan, for her funeral … but I'm stuck," I say. I can feel Harriet's eyes boring into my skin, but I refuse to look over at her.

"Well, that's OK, I tell you what…" Mr Hamilton stands up and walks over to Miss Clarke, and I can see them talking quietly and looking over at me, and Miss Clarke is nodding. It's black dungarees dotted with bright yellow sunflowers today.

Miss Clarke comes over to me, gently puts her hand on my shoulder and says in a quiet voice, "James, do you want to come with me and we can work outside together on your poem?"

Last year Miss Wilson used to boom across the classroom, "James! Would you come here NOW and go through this maths with me, please?" and it would be so embarrassing walking across the room with everyone watching.

But it's not like that in Mr Hamilton's class. I nod and Miss Clarke whisks me out of the classroom before anyone, except Harriet, sees. Finally, I'm out and I breathe a sigh of relief. I'm so glad to be away from everyone.

Miss Clarke and I sit at a table in the school library. Miss Cleveland is our school librarian and she's turned our little library into a place of escape and calm and imagination. There are comfy cushions and beanbags, and everything's tidy and quiet. I instantly feel myself relax a little, surrounded by all the books. Miss Cleveland isn't here today, so it's just me and Miss Clarke.

"So, what's up?" she asks.

Some boys keep saying I'm gay.

My dad thinks I'm gay and hates me.

I might be gay.

My nan died because I'm selfish.

My friends can't stand being around me.

"I wanted to write a poem about my nan, about our memories together, but I'm stuck and I can't do it, and I don't want to let my dad down because he asked me to write something for her funeral, and…" I stop because I've run out of breath.

"OK, we can work on that together. Why don't you show me what you've got?" asks Miss Clarke kindly.

I show her my page, with so many scribbles and crossings out:

I had a nan
And she liked jam...

(not actually true)

My nan is dead
And it hurts my head...

(this IS true)

Miss Clarke reads my "work". Surprisingly, she doesn't roar with laughter and race back into the classroom and read it out to everyone.

"I just can't think," I say, feeling frustrated with myself.

"That's OK, don't worry," says Miss Clarke. "Maybe you're trying too hard to make it rhyme ... or maybe you're just not ready to write it yet. We could talk about your memories of your nan first, and I could write them down for you?"

I nod.

But nothing comes, and I sit there, staring into space. I can't say anything, can't say the words. I don't *want* to remember.

Miss Clarke waits patiently, and I finally shake my

head and say, "I can't... I can't think of anything..."

"It's tough, isn't it? When someone dies you want to remember them and laugh and smile at the memories, but I suppose that would mean accepting that they're gone. Does that make sense?" Miss Clarke says.

My leg starts to jiggle and shake, and I can feel a burning-hot sensation in my chest. Everything aches, and I can't speak.

"We could," Miss Clarke continues, "draw some pictures of what you used to do with her?"

"OK," I whisper.

At first, I don't know what to draw, but a memory of Nan laughing in the kitchen with me while sunlight streamed in through the window dances into my mind, and I shakily start to draw.

I draw pictures of us dancing together and going on the bus to the shops and celebrating birthdays and watching television and eating sweets and cold chocolate from the fridge, but none of my drawings look right.

None of them seem to capture what it is I'm trying to say.

So, nervously, I begin to write. By the end of the lesson I have the first two lines of my poem:

I shall put in my treasure chest of memories
the day we sat in the garden, eating sandwiches
and chocolate from the fridge.
Next, I'll place in it all the times we danced
and laughed together in the kitchen.

I can't write any more down, not yet. It feels too painful, too final.

But the words are there, waiting for me to be ready. And that's a start.

CHAPTER 22

I really do wish I could tell you that my weekend was *full-on*, a totally wild roller coaster of fun. That I went to the cinema and ice-skating and bowling and had friends over and, like, "chilled out" and "hung out" and was all trendy and grown up.

Sadly, it's still Saturday morning and the prospect of another tiresome weekend stretches ahead of me. My Mariah Carey ban hasn't lasted long, and I've already worked my way through her slick, cool, I-just-don't-care-about-anyone album, *Caution*.

Mimi might not care, but I do.

About everything.

I could ring Harriet and see if she wants to do something. But, as much as we try, things don't feel right. There seems to be an agreement between us all to just pretend that the incident with Paul didn't happen.

Why does Harriet always have to make a scene anyway? Why is her answer to everything to "have a word with them" or "beat them up"?

It's Billy in reception all over again. Billy's left our school now, but he was the kind of kid teachers would probably call *energetic* and *determined*. Billy had a habit in reception of pushing all the other kids and laughing at them, and he'd take our toys and refuse to share anything. There was a little doll I absolutely loved in the role-play area, and as soon as he saw me with it, Billy just had to have it! That kind of kid.

I think back to one particularly hot, sunny day when we were on the field and it was all so exciting! We were running around and doing cartwheels, making daisy chains, picking buttercups and just dripping in sweat, so hot and tired. Paul wasn't even on my radar then, and I had none of the worries or hang-ups I have now. When we were called in for lunch, Harriet and I raced to the front of the line, and we were so proud that we were first! There really is something exhilarating about being first in line at school when you're five years old; you feel so grown up and responsible!

So, there we were, looking all smart and regal and ready to lead the class into lunch, and Billy came over. He shoved me out of the way so he was the first in line.

Oh, the injustice! The absolute injustice.

I tapped Billy on the shoulder and said, "Erm … Billy, I was first. You can go behind Harriet."

But Billy just laughed in my face and ignored me.

Exasperated and at a complete loss for what to do, I turned round and looked at Harriet.

And wow! Harriet was fuming. Absolutely fuming! Tiny, five-year-old Harriet was red in the face, her hair slick with sweat and stuck to her forehead, and she was breathing like a charging, angry bull.

"Oi! Billy! James and me were first! Move it!" Harriet yelled, stamping her foot.

But Billy just laughed again, spinning around and around on the spot.

The next thing that Harriet did is the stuff of legend, and probably one of the reasons why no one messes with her.

Harriet glared at Billy and slowly, very slowly, opened her lunch box. Her little cucumber and hummus sandwiches were sealed in a plastic Ziploc bag thing – you know the type – and she removed the sandwiches from the bag, never once taking her eyes off Billy.

He was still spinning around and around in a circle, chanting, "I'm first! I'm first!"

I remember thinking, *What is Harriet doing?*

Harriet put her hand in the plastic sandwich bag so it fit over her hand like a glove. And then she marched over to the corner of the field where none of us were allowed to go. She was muttering to herself, and I saw her bend over and rip something out of the ground, and then turn around and stomp back to the lunch line. Other kids were still joining the queue with their lunch boxes, panting and puffing with the heat.

I saw Harriet and thought, *Oh, why has she picked a big bunch of weeds?*

But before I realized what she was doing, she strode up to Billy, brandishing her weeds.

She shouted, "Oi, Billy!"

He turned around and – it happened so quickly – Harriet slapped him across the face with this bouquet of weeds, and suddenly Billy let out the most horrified, pained scream I'd ever heard.

It was then that I realized that Harriet didn't just

have a bunch of weeds in her hand. No, no. They were stinging nettles.

Stinging nettles! Harriet had just smacked Billy around the face with a huge bunch of prickly, bristly, spiky, spiny *stinging nettles*!

Now, please, please: do not try this at home, kids. Because it did not end well for young Harriet. Oh no.

There was absolute chaos. I was just standing there, eyes wide in shock; Billy was on the ground, screaming and writhing in pain; and Harriet was standing over him, triumphant. She dumped the nettles and ungloved her hand, throwing the plastic sandwich bag to one side. I could see her hand was a tiny bit red and sore, but Harriet didn't seem to care.

Harriet looked at Billy on the ground, and then at me, shrugged, and said, "Well, he won't push in front of us again, will he?"

I remember being terrified. Terrified and *thrilled* by Harriet. Terrified and thrilled and amazed. What a girl! Harriet really is the most brilliant friend you could ask for.

Fierce, loyal, brave.

And, yes, absolutely terrifying.

Anyway, Harriet was hauled into Mrs Garcia's office and got in SO much trouble. But as she was taken away by a shocked midday assistant, Harriet turned around and she smiled at me.

She smiled *and winked*.

And that's when I knew that Harriet would always have my back.

So, it's very on-brand of her to go over to Paul and shout at him and square up to him. I know that. I do. She did what she thought was best. She's a fighter.

But I hate that it drew attention to me. Like, on Tuesday, when she shoved Paul, I felt like she was proving Paul right – proving that I am weak and worthless, and can't defend myself. If only she could have listened to me and let me sort it out myself.

But what would I have done?

Maybe I'm just cross at myself because I've done nothing. I *should* stand up to Paul. Properly stand up to him. Not just "oh please leave me alone". No. Dad always says, "If someone hits you, you hit them back."

But there must be some other way to deal with all this? I just want to be left alone to dance and sing and write poems. To write my poem for Nan.

I'm deep in thought, and Mariah's voice is swishing and whirling around my bedroom, so I jump a little when I hear the doorbell go.

I can see Dad out in the garden already, desperately trying to tidy up our sad rectangle of dry, bare grass. He's trying to keep busy, I know he is. Trying to avoid his ludicrous gay son. Trying to forget Nan.

I sigh and plod downstairs.

It's probably Auntie Kathy and Weird Bruce come to help Dad with the funeral planning.

I fix a great big smile on my face. *It's showtime, James! Everything's fine, honestly!*

So, when I open the door and see Joel standing there, I'm taken aback.

"Why are you grinning like that?" Joel asks, raising an eyebrow.

"Oh, hi, Joel."

My big, fake smile immediately drops, and I look at my feet.

What is he doing here?

"Charming! Glad I came over!" Joel bursts out laughing. He holds his chest, like he's just been struck in the heart with an arrow, and I can't help but giggle.

"Sorry, I meant 'Hi, Joel, how AMAZING to see you!'" I say, grinning.

"That's more like it," he says. He's wearing muddy walking boots, jeans and a dark blue waterproof cagoule. "So, look. I know you're having a rough time at the moment. I thought we could go out with each other today." He blushes and continues, nervously, "Not out-out, not as in going out with each other, just … out. As in go out. Somewhere. Sorry, look: do you want to come for a walk with me?"

He stands there, looking expectantly at me.

Could I do that?

Paul won't see. It's the weekend. It'll be fine.

"A walk would be nice," I say apprehensively. "Yeah, cool. I can do that. Let me just go and tell Dad. Wait there."

I run back along the hall, shove my best trainers on, rush out to the back door and yell up the garden, "Dad! I'm just going for a walk with Nathan!"

Dad looks up from his weeding and seems relieved that I'm finally speaking to him again. He shouts back, "Nathan! Great! Take your phone and be back in an hour! We need to go to Nan's and do some tidying!"

I give him a thumbs up and run back through the hallway. I quickly check my messy hair in the mirror and give it a little zhuzh up. Not bad!

And then I'm back at the front door, where Joel

is still standing, smiling. The thing I always notice about Joel is how still he is, how grounded. I'm always rushing and running and shifting and shuffling and moving, moving, moving, and Joel?

Joel just stands. Quietly and confidently.

"Ready?" Joel asks.

"Ready!" I pant back.

CHAPTER 23

"So, where are we going, then?" I ask Joel as we walk side by side. It's a beautiful, bright, hazy autumn morning.

"Well, we just need to turn here … *this* way." Joel gestures to an overgrown path.

"Are you going to try and murder me?" I ask, laughing. "Because I once did a tae kwon do class and will beat you up!"

"Oh, really?" Joel guffaws, like the idea of me beating anyone up is very funny.

It is, I'm not going to lie.

"No, I'm not going to murder you."

He keeps walking, and we leave the houses and roads behind us, following long-forgotten pathways, until we reach an old wooden gate. It's wrapped in ivy, and as Joel opens it there's a creak, and I realize that we are now properly in the woods.

It's quiet and still, and there is a blanket of rust-coloured leaves on the damp ground. Jewelled cobwebs shine with the morning dew. As we walk further into the woods it smells fragrant – somehow both fresh and ancient. We are surrounded by oranges, browns and bright, vivid reds.

Joels turns and grins at me. "I come here quite a bit. No one seems to know about these woods; they're always empty..." He looks up towards the sky, and the sun filters through the archway of trees, making his face glow.

"I used to come here after we moved house, just to get my head together," Joel continues. "It was ... a lot. A lot to deal with."

I nod, not quite sure what to say. Should I ask him about it? Does he want to talk?

"Almost there," Joel says, clapping his hands together.

We continue walking through the woods and he's right, there's no one here. It's peaceful and silent.

Finally, Joel stops and says, "Here we are."

I gasp because there, in front of us, is a stream weaving through the trees. The sunlight bounces off the crystal-clear water and the trickling, babbling current seems to talk and laugh.

"This is … wow … it's beautiful," I say.

The woods feel magical. Joel sits down on a damp fallen tree trunk.

"Come and sit down," Joel says, shuffling along.

I sit down uncomfortably next to him and tap my fingers on my legs, nervous and unsure.

"So, what do we do now?" I ask, fidgeting and looking around.

"Nothing," says Joel. His eyes are still closed, and there's a tiny smile creeping across his face. "Just sit. Just listen."

"Oh, right," I say. "Yep, I can do that. I've never actually been here, by the way. Not once. Didn't even know all this was here! But then again, I'm not really an outdoors kind of lad, I—"

"Ssshhhhhh," Joel says, opening one eye and chuckling. "You don't need to talk or entertain me. Just sit."

The wood is lovely; dark and deep. It is a brambly wilderness, and as I close my eyes and take a few deep breaths I feel myself relaxing, slowing down.

I listen.

I hear the wings of a dragonfly *frrripp* overhead.

I pay attention to the stream as it chatters over the stones and gravel. I listen to the rustle of the leaves. To the chitter-chatter and singing of the birds. The scurrying of squirrels. The trees seem to whisper, the oak trees standing guard over us. I drink it all in and let it wash over me, almost like a song. A quiet, healing song of hope.

I think about Nan.

And I think about the woods.

The woods seem to know that death is not the end.

Every year they lose their leaves, watch them drifting and dancing on to the ground. I wonder if they're sad, if they feel lost and lonely when they say goodbye, when their leaves wither and fall.

I think about how every year the trees seem to die.

But then I think about how they begin again, how life begins again when spring comes and everything starts anew.

I wonder if anything or anyone ever really dies or if life just carries on, again and again, renewing. It's a comforting thought, the circle of life. That Nan, like the autumn leaves and the bare trees, will begin again, somewhere, somehow. That I might be able to find her in the cool shade of the woods or in the whisper of the trees or the tinkling, soothing laughter of the stream or the—

"I need to tell you something…" Joel says, his voice interrupting my daydream.

"Shhhhhhhhh!" I say, and laugh, my eyes closed. "No talkin', remember!"

"It's just that—"

"Please, Joel," I say, opening my eyes. "Not today. Not now. I just want to sit and listen. Please."

"OK," Joel whispers.

We stay there for a long time, until it starts to drizzle, and I sigh because I know it's over, it's time to go back.

We begin our journey home.

On the walk back, neither Joel nor I speak. We don't have to.

When we reach my front door, I turn to Joel and whisper, "Thank you."

"Any time," he says. He seems at peace, serene. "I'll see you at school on Monday."

And with that he turns and walks away, and I stand at the door, watching him.

CHAPTER 24

"Hi, James…"

I'm sitting on the bench in the playground with my eyes closed, trying to recapture some of those emotions, some of that quiet calm I felt in the woods with Joel on Saturday.

But it's been hard. I've had to keep peeking to make sure Paul hasn't snuck up on me.

I can hear Harriet and Joel laughing and chatting with Summer, Harry and Ohrim. Neither of them has ventured far away from me, even though I said I was fine and just wanted to sit quietly.

"Erm … James…"

I open my eyes and see Sandra in Year 5 standing in front of me, shuffling from one foot to the other like a fluffy, excited bunny. This is very unlike her!

What does she want? And where's Nathan? Why aren't they wandering around, giggling and batting their eyelashes at each other? Aren't they joined at the hip?

"Ihadacat," she blurts out.

"Oh. Erm … OK!" I say. I'm not sure why Sandra in Year 5 is here and why she's telling me she had a cat. Is this some sort of prank?

Do not engage with her, James.

Sandra in Year 5's still shuffling, but now she's chewing on the end of her jumper sleeve too. "She died," she continues. "She was like my little shadow. And I heard about your nan, and I wanted to say sorry, because when my cat died, I felt really sad."

"My nan dying and your cat dying isn't really the same thing," I say, bristling with irritation.

But I immediately feel bad.

What is wrong with me? She's obviously just trying to be nice.

"Sorry," I mutter.

Sandra sits down on the bench next to me. "That's OK, and I didn't mean your nan dying was like my cat dying because my dad says she was just a cat. But … she was *my* cat, you know?"

I turn to look at her and see she's looking down

at the ground, her red hair hanging over her face.

"She was called Lola, and she was black and sleek, and when I saw her for the first time I thought she was so beautiful! She strutted everywhere and used to like lying in the road sunbathing. It was so funny! My dad said she was brainless and would get run over one day."

She turns to look at me, and I wonder why she's telling me all this.

"But she didn't get run over. She got poorly, really quickly, and I tried…"

Sandra stops for a second. I think maybe I should hug her or pat her hand or something, but I don't.

"I tried to make her better, and I used my pocket money to get her special cat food so she had something nice to eat, but … erm… Well, the vet said she was really ill and we had to have her put down." The end of Sandra's jumper is soggy where she's been chewing on it. "I felt really bad afterwards, like it was all my fault, like I should have found a way to save her, or seen she was sick sooner, and I just thought you might feel bad too about your nan and I wanted … I wanted to say I hope you can remember the happy, nice times with her. When I miss Lola, I try and remember when she sat on my bed and I'd read to her, or when she woke me up by sitting on my head, or…"

It seems for a moment like she can't go on, and I think I understand what she's saying, and I realize how kind it was of her to come over to me because we're not even friends.

"Anyway, I should go before Nathan… I should get going!" Sandra looks shyly at me and brushes her red hair out of her eyes.

"I'm sorry about your cat … about Lola," I say.

She nods and pats my hand quickly, then wanders across the playground to meet Nathan.

In the afternoon we have PE. I never used to mind PE as I've always been pretty good at gymnastics, and dance, and rounders. This has always annoyed Paul, who seems to think that *he's* the only one who can be good at sport and that I can't possibly be good at it too.

But now we're in Year 6, the boys and girls get changed in different rooms. The girls get changed in a Year 3 classroom while the Year 3 children are swimming, and the boys get changed in our classroom.

I *hate* getting changed now. It feels really unsafe to be getting undressed with all the other boys around. Most of the time Miss Clarke supervises the girls and

Mr Hamilton waits outside our classroom, by the door, to give us some privacy, I suppose. It just means that Paul can make little digs and sly comments about me without anyone hearing.

I try to get changed as quickly as I can so that I can wait outside near Mr Hamilton. Last week, Paul told everyone that I was watching him get changed and I *wasn't*. I just made the mistake of looking up, instead of looking down the whole time. How dare I?!

Next, Paul will say I shouldn't be in the same room with them, and it seems horrible that something as simple as getting changed should become scary.

Today, as I'm hurrying to tie the drawstring on my shorts, I see that Nathan is struggling to undo his laces. They're full of knots and badly tangled.

Come on, James. Be the bigger person.

"Do you want some help?" I ask. Maybe this will be the moment he starts speaking to me again? He'll remember what a good friend I am!

Nathan ignores me, looks down at his shoes, and carries on picking and tugging at his laces.

"Nathan? Do you want some help?" I repeat.

"No, no. Just stop talking to me, please!" Nathan begs.

I've had enough of this. It's so ridiculous – we were

such good mates! "What is going on?" I ask. "Why won't you talk to me?"

Joel has got changed and is standing next to Nathan, looking angry.

"Just tell him," Joel insists.

"I can't be friends with you any more…" Nathan whispers, glancing around.

"What? Why not?" I say, and I sound desperate. "We've been friends for ages!"

Nathan looks at the floor. He seems torn between being embarrassed and sorry, but also scared and nervous, like talking to me is going to get him in trouble.

"Because … because…" He looks at Joel, and Joel glares at him. "Because Paul says you're gay and if anyone talks to you, they're gay too."

"Not that it would be an issue if anyone was gay," Joel snaps at Nathan, shaking his head in disgust.

My heart drops. "That's *so* ludicrous!" I say and try and laugh, but I can see that Nathan doesn't think it is.

"Nathan, you're ridiculous," snaps Joel, "so immature."

"He's … he's set up a WhatsApp group with some of the boys in the class and he's saying stuff about you on there…" Nathan says, finally managing to undo his laces. His PE top is on back to front and inside out. He starts to put his plimsolls on.

Suddenly it all makes sense! I realize why so many of my classmates won't speak to me any more! Why so many of the boys are whispering about me behind my back. First it was Jake, then Riyad and Archie, and then Rafe ... Rafe, of all people, has stopped speaking to me! I've always thought of him as being like a bouncy golden retriever, so happy and excitable. It's not like we were best mates, but he's always spoken to me in the playground and cheered at our dances and asked me how Mariah's getting on. But now even Rafe has been trying to avoid me.

I realize all this and I feel sick with shame.

I turn to Joel, remembering that night we were all round Harriet's house. They were whispering about a WhatsApp group and I knew, I just *knew*, something was going on.

"How long have you known about this?" I ask, taking a step around my desk, so I'm closer to him now. I can see the anger in Joel's face transform into worry.

We were together, at the weekend. We were in the woods together and ... is *this* what he was trying to tell me in the woods?

But you didn't want to know, James. He tried to tell you. He did.

"We just thought it was best you didn't find out," Joel says, pleading with me.

"WE?" I exclaim, and I wonder how many people know about this group. I feel so stupid!

"Me and … erm … Harriet," says Joel, and he winces as he says it, like he's in pain.

"*Harriet?*" I say, spitting out her name. "You and Harriet KNEW and you didn't tell me?"

Joel looks nervous, and I'm not surprised. I can feel my blood boiling and my face going red. I don't care that everyone has stopped getting changed and is staring at us.

I can see Paul smirking from the corner of my eye.

"I'm sorry," Joel whispers, and he really does look it, but it's too late now for me. I feel my nostrils flare and my eyes narrow. I feel like I've gone past the point of return and am speeding towards something explosive.

I don't think I can control myself.

And, sure enough, before I realize what I'm doing, I move around my desk and, without thinking, I push Joel.

I push him really, really hard and he slams back into his desk.

He looks shocked and is about to say something when Paul hoots with laughter and shouts, "Oh, look! Jamesssss and Joel are having a lovers' tiff! They're going to break up!"

Paul has finally turned on Joel too, and it's all my fault.

"SHUT UP!" Joel screams at Paul, and as I'm moving towards him for another push, Joel launches himself across the classroom at Paul.

But he doesn't get to him before Mr Hamilton comes into the classroom.

"Boys? What's all the noise about?"

He waits.

"Joel?" Mr Hamilton asks.

Joel looks at me, and I shake my head.

"Nothing, Mr Hamilton," Joel says. "It's nothing."

Mr Hamilton sighs. "Well, come on then! You need to get changed now!"

It's enough to make us all stop, and it defuses the situation. And it's a good job, because I would have pushed Joel again and again. And I think Joel would have beaten Paul up, he seemed that angry.

As we start lining up for PE, Joel grabs my hand and whispers, "James, I'm sorry, all right? We were trying to protect you!"

But I shake his hand off me and whisper, "Get off me, you GAYBOY! I don't want anything to do with you."

Joel looks like I've slapped him round the face.

And I feel sick. I hate myself for it.

I know, deep down, that it's not Joel's fault, or Harriet's, but I feel betrayed. They're meant to have my back, to tell me when something's going on, *not* hide secrets from me. All this time, Paul and his awful, *awful* friends have been messaging about me behind my back.

And Nathan won't speak to me because *Paul* says he can't? Do all the years of friendship mean nothing to him? I wonder why some kids in the class have so much power and why some of us feel so powerless and small.

What can I do about the WhatsApp group? No one can help me with that. It's happening outside of school and has nothing to do with the teachers, surely? Should I ignore it?

Ignoring things hasn't been going well for me recently.

We are led out to PE, and I see Harriet give me a small wave. But I glare at her and shake my head and look away.

That's it. I'm done with them all now. My friends are liars and I can't trust them.

I realize that I don't know how to deal with any of this.

I have no one to talk to or turn to any more.

I am alone.

I Was Nathan

I was your friend,
But now I shun and ignore you.
I was your champion,
But now my cheers are slivers of icy silence.
I was your keeper of secrets,
But now I whisper lies and untruths.
I was your safety net,
But now that net strangles and suffocates.
I was close, just like a brother,
But now the distance between us is too far.
I was Nathan.
But now you ask: were you, really?

CHAPTER 25

As soon as school ends, I stomp out of the gates. I hear Joel and Harriet shouting at me to wait, but I don't ever want to speak to them again.

All this time, *all this time*, people have been laughing at me behind my back. The silly gay boy with the silly voice and the silly dreams to write songs with Mariah Carey!

Even my so-called friends have been lying to me.

My mind is racing, and I want to punch someone or something SO hard. Paul's stupid potato face floats in my mind and I want to punch and punch and punch until there's nothing left in me.

I shove my headphones into my ears and play my favourite Mariah songs. Songs about being brave and facing your fears and making things happen in your life and going for it.

But it all seems so stupid, so babyish. What is the point?

Because it's not Paul any more. There are more of them.

I can't tell them to stop talking about me and messaging about me. I used to think it was just this awful thing that happened at school, that I was safe outside school, but I realize it's not. Even at home, it's like Paul's ominous presence has been hovering over me. Even when I've been relaxing or reading or singing or dancing in my room, they've been talking about me. Judging me and laughing at me, like I'm completely worthless.

A joke. The class joke.

And I'm done in. Completely exhausted.

Do not cry, James. Don't give them the satisfaction.

I sit on Nan's wall for a bit, knees hunched up to my chin.

She would know what to do. She would. If she'd known how bad it had become, she'd have run down to the school *so* fast no one would have been able to catch her. And she would have grabbed Paul and shaken him until he was crying, and everyone would have been laughing because a little old lady had embarrassed Paul and made *him* feel worthless.

I'm deep in thought, plotting every kind of revenge on Paul imaginable, when I hear a yap and a bark. It's Miss Fluffy, and Ruth and Eliana are there.

Ruth smiles at me, but something seems different today, and I can't work out what.

"Hi, James," says Ruth. "Are you OK?"

She looks alarmed now, and I realize that I must look like a complete mess – *a very sorry sight indeed*, as Nan would say.

"Bit of a rubbish start to the week," I say.

"Want to talk about it?" asks Ruth. She sits down next to me on the wall.

And then I realize what's different about them.

"You're not holding hands!" I blurt out. They always hold hands.

"Erm, no … not today," says Eliana.

"Why not?"

It seems easier to ask about their problems than talk about mine. Maybe they've had an argument and I can help. It would be nice to feel helpful.

"Just some people around here, shouting some horrible things at us," says Ruth.

Eliana looks at her as if to say, *Be quiet! He's only a kid! He might explode if we tell him the truth!*

"I'm sorry," I say. "People are rubbish." If Ruth and Eliana can't even hold hands, there's no reason to believe it will ever get better for me.

Ruth laughs. "Yes, yes, they are rubbish, I'm afraid. But we'll be back to normal soon. It just took us by surprise, that's all. We thought we were past all *this*. And don't think we haven't noticed how you haven't answered my question, James," Ruth continues gently. "Come on, what's happened?"

What can I say?

Everyone hates me and they all think I'm gay and I don't know if I am and my friends have been lying to me and I don't feel safe and I miss my nan and everywhere I go I feel worried and anxious and scared that someone's going to say something or push me or whisper my name or make me feel rubbish and my dad won't talk to me about my nan and he hates it whenever I talk about Joel. And Joel! I called him a gayboy. I'm just as bad as Paul and Jake and...

And all of it seems too much, and at the same time so pointless and whiny and pathetic. Little gay boy gets bullied. It's the oldest story in the book, and I don't want that story for me.

So, I settle with, "I'm just really, really angry. Even my Mariah music's not helping today!" I think back to the time I ripped up her poster and realize I've been angry for a long, long time.

Ruth and Eliana look at each other and smile. It's that "I know exactly what you're thinking" kind of smile. Ruth jumps up and Miss Fluffy barks and farts again.

"Come on, James!" Ruth laughs. "Up you get! Come with us!"

So, despite Dad telling me that they're strangers, and years of warnings about not getting into cars with strangers and not taking sweets from strangers, I follow them a few doors down from Nan's to their house. They don't look like serial killers, but you never can tell. They lead me down the side of their house, and Miss Fluffy jumps up at me excitedly.

"Stop it! Down, Princess!" Eliana says sharply.

So, her name is Princess!

It's a name that suits her. I imagine she's quite a handful and very demanding. In my mind, I see her lying on a chaise longue, barking orders at Eliana and Ruth— *Oh, barking orders! Ha!* I chuckle at my little joke, and feel a bit better, for a moment, like everything at school and home is forgotten, like it's happening to someone else.

At the back of their house is a garage. We don't have a garage, so I've always wondered what people keep in theirs. Swimming pools? Dead bodies? Secret alien laboratories? Maybe even a sound booth for recording songs! I could write a song for Mariah and send it to her!

No, James. Stop being weird!

But as they winch up the door of their garage, I see that Eliana and Ruth's garage is very different. It's like a fancy gym! There's a bike and a running machine and weights and a punchbag. I wander around touching things and going, "Wow! What's this?" a lot because I've never been in a gym; they always seem to be grunty, sweaty places. But not here; here, there's a big inflatable ball that I sit on, and bounce up and down, and even Eliana laughs.

"OK, so let's get some gloves on you," Ruth says, and she puts these huge gloves on me, the ones that boxers wear. They're red and white and I feel very cool indeed. Wasn't Mariah's video for "Triumphant" shot in a boxing ring? And didn't she wear gold boxing gloves to fight her arch-nemesis Bianca during the Rainbow World Tour?

A spark. A glimmer returning?

"I thought you might like to have a go on the

punchbag," Ruth continues. "Give it a hit and get some of that anger out."

It feels like a strange thing to do, and I've never hit a punchbag, but I say, "Thank you."

"We'll be inside, so just pop by when you're done," says Ruth, and they leave me there, standing looking at the big punchbag hanging from a chain in the ceiling.

I give it a little push and it's *heavy* and hardly swings at all.

This is absurd, I tell myself, giving the punchbag another shove. But this time it feels a bit better, and so I give it a gentle hit with my right fist. I circle round the punch bag a few times, feeling light and speedy, giving it a few more taps and jabs.

I hit the bag hard this time, and my fist smarts from the impact. But it feels good.

So, I hit it again and again. While I hit, I think about Nathan and everything he's done and everything we've lost. Do real friends really treat you like that? What has happened to him?

And then, then I imagine the punchbag is Paul, or Dad, or the people who made Ruth and Eliana feel scared to hold hands. I imagine it's Mr Hamilton and think of his troublesome project.

And then it's Mrs Gallagher with her permission slip.

Smack.

Duck!

Hit.

Duck!

Punch.

It's like a dance!

I think of Harriet's face, and Joel's, too, and I hit harder and harder, each punch coming breathlessly, messily, and full of anger.

You don't keep secrets from your friends, you just don't!

I imagine it's me, the boy who pushed Joel and called him a "gayboy".

GAY.

GAY.

GAY.

HIT!

HIT!

HIT!

Sweat is dripping down my face and my hair is stuck to my forehead, but I keep going. For every mistake, every put-down, every insult, every time I've been made to feel less than or like I don't fit in, I hit.

I hit for my nan too, for all the rage, and fear,

and regret that she's gone, and that she's left me here with no one. And with every punch, a roar, a scream leaves my body, from somewhere deep down. The punches keep coming until I'm completely and utterly exhausted.

I finally collapse on the floor, shaking, dizzy and hot. My school shirt is stuck to my body, and I feel better. The ache in my chest is still there, but while I was punching and hitting it was like I couldn't focus on anything else. Like all my frustration finally had somewhere to go.

I sit for a while on the floor of the garage, panting hard and taking sips from the water bottle in my school bag. I wrap my arms tightly around myself and rock backwards and forwards. I feel like I could fall asleep here.

Eventually, as the street lights start to come on, I can smell garlic and spices being cooked from the house next door, and I drag myself off the floor. I walk round to the front of the house and knock on the door.

I feel … it's weird, but I feel drained and tired … but also full of energy too.

Ruth comes and opens the door. "How did you get on?" she asks, smiling at my sweaty, bedraggled state.

"It was *good*, thank you," I say.

"I'm glad it was useful. You can come back any time you want, James," Ruth says.

I nod and say thank you and politely say no when she asks if I'd like to come in for a cup of tea or something to eat.

Dad wouldn't like that.

And besides, I need to go home.

I need to go home and I need to write Nan's poem.

CHAPTER 26

Dad doesn't come home from work until late, and then goes straight to Nan's to carry on clearing the house out, so I spend the evening in my room. Auntie Kathy and Weird Bruce are downstairs "babysitting" me while Dad is out. They're watching a horrible, rowdy game show and cackling loudly.

I pretend I have a headache so I can avoid them and write Nan's poem.

I haven't had much faith in myself recently, but sometimes you just have to start – to have faith that you can write.

So, where do I begin?

I lie on my bed, close my eyes and take a deep breath. I think of the boxing in Ruth's garage. I think of the woods, where I felt so calm and peaceful. I try not to think of Joel being there, but just focus on the soothing silence. I think of Mariah and her resilience and strength. I think of "I Don't Wanna Cry" and of "If It's Over" and "A No No" and of "Almost Home", and how she got back up every time she was knocked down.

I pick up my pen and notepad, just like Mariah in the "Bye Bye" video.

I am ready.

I begin to write.

I write quickly, breathlessly. I don't check back over what I've written. I don't reread the poem. I write about everything Nan meant to me, meant to us. I write and I write until I'm completely drained and fall asleep.

I wake up an hour later. I can still hear the TV blaring downstairs and Weird Bruce roaring with laughter.

I sit up and cross my legs and nervously reread Nan's poem.

And you know what? It's not bad! It's not a complete disaster.

It's just a shame the rest of my life is a complete and utter disaster. Where do I even start with *that*?

AARRGGHH! It's all so confusing!

In the morning, I decide that I'm going to try and talk to my friends, and I'm going to say sorry. This will be the day everything falls into place!

But, just before the bell goes, I see Joel and Harriet walking into the playground, whispering and looking at me, and I feel that swell of anger all over again.

Where's that punchbag when I need it?

I stare at them in disgust. What do those two have to whisper about? Maybe they've joined Paul's stupid WhatsApp group, and maybe they're spreading rumours about me too? Well, that's just fine, if they're going to be like that! Suddenly I don't want to say sorry, and I don't want to "be the bigger person". Why should I?

So, when Harriet starts walking towards me, I turn the other way.

Take that, Harriet!

The day passes painfully. Joel and I work on our "Famous Faces Throughout History" project all afternoon, but it's horrible, because I really do want to speak to him, and underneath it all, I'm desperate for everything to be OK again between us.

I want to see Joel smile and see those green eyes sparkle again.

But when Joel sits down next to me, he won't look at me. He just says, "Do you want to carry on writing the introduction, and I'll do the definitions of what all the letters mean in 'LGBTQ+'?"

I nod and say snarkily, "I don't care. Do whatever you want," and Joel just shakes his head.

What is wrong with me? Until I found out about the WhatsApp group, he'd been so nice to me, and I was so excited about working with him and getting to know him more, and I loved that he'd become part of our friendship group.

But Joel lied to me.

So, the afternoon passes slowly, and I hardly write anything. Whenever Paul gets up to sharpen his pencil, or get some more paper, or borrow an iPad for research, he walks by my seat and whispers, "Jaaammessss…" It makes me flinch every time. Sometimes he kicks my chair legs so it jolts me. Joel glares at him, and I can see that his hands are gripping the desk, his knuckles white.

In a way, I'd rather Paul just walked up to me and punched me right in the face. Wouldn't it be so much easier? And it would all be over quickly. But this feels like an endless attack, grinding me down every day.

I was so ready to face everything and started the day feeling so brave, my gold boxing gloves metaphorically ready to go. But once again I say nothing. I just stare ahead, pretending it's happening to someone else.

And I don't miss the irony when I'm finding out about Marsha P. Johnson and all these pioneers, warriors and trailblazers in the LGBTQ+ community, that their achievements haven't exactly helped me out, have they? Who cares about riots and protests and people fighting for equality and freedom when it's still happening today? When kids are still whispered about and pushed and called "gay" and shunned and ignored and treated like they mean nothing – what was the point of it all?

"James, could you stay behind, please?"

My stomach flips because it's the end of the day on Wednesday and these are *not* the words I want to hear … ever!

Mr Hamilton must see the expression on my face because he says, "Don't worry, you're not in any trouble! Just wait here and I'll see the rest of the class out."

What follows is an agonizing seven thousand

hours of waiting. OK, maybe it's, like, ten minutes, but it *feels* longer. Dad always used to say, "I've told you one *million* times not to exaggerate", and he'd laugh afterwards.

I'm looking through the books in our Book Corner – I realize I haven't read much lately – when I hear a familiar voice. And I think, *No way, it can't be. It CAN'T be!* But it is, and as much as I can't believe it and don't want it to be happening, Mr Hamilton is walking into the classroom, chatting away, and DAD is walking in sullenly behind him. DAD!

Maybe Mr Hamilton's invited him in because I've done some GREAT work and he wants to share it? Yes! He sometimes does that, you know! He'll ring a kid's parents and tell them how polite or kind their kid has been. Harriet said he rung her mum once to say that she was the best footballer in Year 6 and would *definitely* be playing for England one day and was *definitely* better than Paul.

I'm not so sure about that last part, but that's what Harriet said.

Mr Hamilton gestures to the chairs, and Dad makes an embarrassing joke about the size of them. They're not even that small! Dad does look funny, though, sitting on a school chair like a naughty boy.

He looks tired, and his face is covered in stubble. He looks at me and raises an eyebrow quizzically, and I realize that he thinks I'm in trouble. My life is pretty much over.

"Hello, Mr Turner," begins Mr Hamilton, and he looks serious. "I just wanted to invite you in today to see how you and James were getting on. I know you've had a rough time lately. I was really sorry to hear about your mother, and your nan, James."

OK, so maybe this is just a standard check-in after someone in your family dies! That must be it! That's thoughtful of Mr Hamilton.

"Erm ... thanks," says Dad gruffly, and I think back to when he went to war with Miss Wilson at Parents' Evening, and how different he is now. He seems so unsure of himself and won't look at Mr Hamilton. Mr Hamilton doesn't seem to notice, or if he does, he doesn't let it stop him.

"So, how is everything? I know you've got the funeral this weekend," he says.

HOW does he know? HOW do teachers know EVERYTHING?

"We're fine," says Dad.

Phew! I reach for my school bag and hope that the conversation is over.

"It's just that James … James doesn't *seem* fine," Mr Hamilton says, and I look at him in shock. *What a traitor!* I'm fine. I AM FINE.

"What do you mean?" Dad asks, looking at me accusingly.

Mr Hamilton looks directly at me then and says, "You just seem, well, not your usual bubbly self. You seem very tired and down, and I've noticed you're struggling to concentrate in class."

"I'm fine," I whisper. "Completely fine."

Maybe not completely fine, Mr Hamilton. More like completely not fine.

"And I've noticed," Mr Hamilton says, gently but firmly, "that you don't seem to be talking to Nathan or Harriet or Joel at the moment, and we're all just worried about you, James."

"Why aren't you speaking to Nathan and Harriet?" Dad asks me.

Mr Hamilton looks at Dad with a furrowed brow, but I don't know why.

"We're just … we're just not speaking at the moment," I say.

But I've changed my mind, Mr Hamilton, I'd like to speak to someone after all. About Nan and Harriet and Nathan and Paul … and Joel…

"OK, fine," snaps Dad. "Thanks for your help, Mr Hamilton. I'll speak to James at home."

"I'm happy to organize someone for James to talk to about things, if you think that would help? Mrs Achebe does some great work in the Sunshine Room," says Mr Hamilton, but Dad is already getting up from the school chair (OK, it does seem impossibly tiny).

"That won't be necessary," says Dad, and then, "but … erm … thank you."

"Perhaps we can catch up in a few weeks, then?" says Mr Hamilton.

Please help us, please help us, Mr Hamilton.

"Perhaps. Come on, James, get your bag."

Mr Hamilton nods sadly at me and watches as I scurry after Dad, who's marching out of the classroom.

We just about get out of the school gates before Dad explodes. "What was THAT about? Not listening? Not concentrating? What is going on, James?"

"Nothing," I mutter.

"Well, that can't be true, can it? Anyway, why aren't you speaking to Harriet? Or Nathan? Do I need to ring their parents or something?"

"NO, Dad! It's fine, I'll sort it with them. We had a silly argument, that's all!" I say.

Then Dad hisses, "Is this about this class project you're working on? The one with Joel? I've seen your notes and the writing in your room—"

Urgh! I thought I'd hidden those so well!

"It's got nothing to do with that, Dad. And don't go into my room!" I just wish he'd talk to me and not shout at me and not blame me for everything and JUST LISTEN.

"Well, it must be something. It's that Joel boy, isn't it? Are people saying things about you? About you and Joel?"

"NO!" I yell. "What's Joel got to do with any of it?"

He knows.

He knows and he hates you.

"You need to make some changes, James," Dad says. "Let's just get through the ... get through the funeral on Saturday and then you need to sort yourself out."

"I just knew it would be my fault!" I say, shaking my head.

"What do you mean? James, what is *going on*? I can't help you if you won't talk to me…"

"It works both ways, Dad," I mutter.

"What did you say?" Dad says slowly.

"Nothing, just leave it. It's fine. *I'm fine.*"

He looks at me for a long time, and then he just shakes his head, sighs, and says, "I'm going to Nan's to finish cleaning the living room."

Of course he is.

I watch Dad turn his back on me and walk away.

CHAPTER 27

"Oi! James, I want to speak to you," Harriet says.

It's Friday and she's standing in front of me in the playground.

Please nothing else, Harriet!

On Thursday morning Mrs Gallagher cornered me and asked about my permission slip for choir. I told her Dad was signing it that very evening and I'd definitely get it back to her by today.

But I couldn't bring myself to ask him. Not after the meeting with Mr Hamilton.

And then during assembly, Paul started kicking the back of my feet over and over again. Then he began to whisper, "Jaaaammmeessss … Jammmeessss…"

And then Jake started whispering my name.

And then Nathan.

Not Nathan, too.

"Jaaaammmeessss … Jammmeessss…"

A tidal wave of spiteful, threatening whispers, low and menacing behind me.

It was petrifying. It seemed to paralyse me, and I just sat, frozen, heart beating, staring forwards, pretending to be really interested in Mrs Garcia's assembly.

So now that it's finally Friday and I've nearly, *nearly* made it to the end of the week, I can't cope with anything else happening.

But here's Harriet: legs planted firmly apart, hands on hips.

She's been trying to talk to me all week. But I just grunted or looked the other way.

I'm sat on the playground bench now, with my notebook, reading through Nan's poem. It's nearly there. Bit sentimental in places, could do with some tightening up and editing towards the end.

But it's nearly there.

So, I really don't want to speak to Harriet right now.

"James? Hello? We need to talk!"

"Harriet," I say, taking a deep, scornful breath, "I'm busy at the moment."

"Yeah, me too! I'm missing football for this!" Harriet snaps back. "But we still need to chat."

"What about? You lied to me! You all lied to me!" I challenge her.

"Yes, we did. And I feel bad," says Harriet, sighing. "We just didn't know what to do, and I just thought it was so … so … urgh! Like, who cares if you're gay?"

"Paul cares. And Nathan. And Riyad. And even Rafe! And all the other boys, who are being weird around me and won't look at me or talk to me. Do you have any idea how embarrassing it is?"

Harriet looks at the ground. "I know. I know, and I'm sorry. And we shouldn't have kept it a secret from you. But … what would you have done, anyway?" she says carefully.

"What do you mean?" I ask.

"Well, you haven't done anything about it at all. You never do anything. We could have told Mr Hamilton, or your dad, or I could have spoken to Paul, or…"

"Or what? Hit him with some stinging nettles?" I snap. "We're not in reception any more, Harriet. I don't need you to save me. I just want it all to go away. I want to be left alone, and I don't need to tell any adults. I'll just be called a telltale or a wimp, or … worse. Just leave it, Harriet."

"Fine! Fine." Harriet holds her hands up.

"And why do you care so much, anyway? You didn't even want to work with me for our project!" *Oh, it's all coming out now!*

Harriet takes a step forward and folds her arms across her chest. She grits her teeth, lowers her voice and says, "You're so selfish, James! Not everything is about you! I thought ... I thought I liked Nathan ... as in *liked* him ... but then he started being horrible to you and saying awful homophobic stuff and..."

WHAT?! It's my turn to drag my eyes away now and look out over the playground to where Nathan is. Harriet is meant to be my best friend, and I didn't know!

Furious at myself for not realizing what's really been happening – yet again! – I say, "Fine. Whatever, Harriet."

"AAARRRGGHHH!" she screams, exasperated. "What is WRONG with you? Why are you ignoring this? It's not going to go away, James. Let's go and tell Mr Hamilton. It's for the best."

"For the best?" I say, standing up. I can feel my temper rising again. "What would you know about what's best for me?"

Harriet looks at me indignantly, so I dare to go further:

"All you've done so far is *make everything worse!*"

I see that flash of vehemence she had on her face when she hit Billy in reception.

"I miss my best friend, James. The old James would never take this. And you…" She sounds incensed now. "You're just a *coward*. You're a coward, and a loser, and Mariah would be ashamed of you."

And then Harriet says something that feels so mean, so unnecessary, that I gasp in shock: "And your nan would be ashamed of you too."

She turns on her heel and runs off towards the school field.

In the distance, I see Joel looking at me.

What have I done?

CHAPTER 28

Saturday morning.

The day of the funeral.

I push aside all thoughts of Harriet and Joel and Nathan. Just for today.

I can't face it today. I can't face the idea that Harriet might be right about me after all. That I am weak and pathetic. That I've done *nothing* to save myself. That I haven't turned up for myself recently.

I push it all down, just until we've said goodbye to Nan.

It's odd because it feels like I've been waiting ages to say goodbye to Nan, but at the same time it feels like it's all come too soon.

I don't want to go, I don't. I don't want to go and

read my poem or say goodbye because all of it means that she's gone and it's not fair.

I just want her back.

So, even though I'm nervous and absolutely *do not* want to go, I'm ready in my shirt and black trousers by nine a.m., a whole three hours before the ceremony. Is it called a ceremony? Isn't that a wedding? My stomach fills with heaviness thinking about Mr Hamilton's wedding, and how I'll have to miss it next weekend...

Dad has spent ages ironing our clothes and I don't want to crease them, so I stand by my window in silence. No Mariah today. It doesn't feel right. I watch the rain pitter and patter on to the grass outside. Everything seems wet and damp and cold.

I've never been to a funeral before. Granddad died when I was very young, and Mum and Dad later explained it wouldn't have been "appropriate" for me to go. It's funny how adults seem to make so many decisions about what's right or wrong for us kids because from what I've seen they don't really have a clue what they're doing any more than we do.

And now I'm in the position of being eleven and never having been to a funeral before, so I don't know what to expect. How do we get to the church? Will

Nan be… Will I be able to *see* Nan? Where do you sit? Or do you stand? Where do I go to read my poem?

Where does she go after?

And what are we supposed to do after it all?

Mum will be there too. I'll have to see Mum, of course.

And I know I could have asked Dad all of this and saved myself a lot of worry, but his mood at the moment is saying "Don't come near me", and I realize – I *know* – how much I've hurt him.

I look up at the blanket of grey clouds and wonder if Nan's up there, and if she's looking down on me. *I know I've mucked up*, I whisper to her, wherever she is. *I know I've hurt Dad and I've been horrible to Harriet and Joel. I know that. But it's been pretty rubbish without you, you know?*

And there are all the *other* feelings that are confusing me. Like, why *do* I still want to smile whenever I see Joel, and why do I hate that we're not speaking, and why do people at school *keep saying* I have a girl's voice and that I'm … *that word*?

Gay. Just say it!

Am I gay?

Maybe they all see something in me that I don't see yet?

And would it be so terrible if I *were* *that word*?

Our project about Marsha P. Johnson has meant I've read about all these other LGBTQ+ people and their lives. I know there are struggles, and I know horrible things are done to them, I know that. I know gay kids get thrown out of their homes too. I know people get beaten up and killed and people say disgusting things about us.

About THEM. Them.

But I also know that there's lots of colour, life and happiness in their community. That people make new families and friends and have fulfilled, amazing lives. Lives that scream "This is me!" Lives full of music and art and passion and love.

And I think Nan would want that for me. She would want me to be happy and brave and fearless and just to be myself, no matter what Paul, or anyone else, says.

I stay standing at the window, watching for a sign, watching for Nan, for a long time. But nothing comes.

The hours pass by, and eventually I hear Dad knock on my door and say quietly, "James ... James, it's time to go..."

I push all these thoughts back down again.

I just have to get through today.

Taking a deep breath, I square my shoulders and get ready to say goodbye to Nan.

"Erm ... hello ... everyone..."

I'm standing at the front of the church, clinging on to the lectern like the ground is going to swallow me.

Just look forward, James.

People are watching me, people who have come to pay their respects to Nan and are waiting for me to speak. But I can't look at them, not yet.

Dad patted my leg before I came up and squeezed my hand, and it's the most contact we've had for such a long time. I can feel my black tie and it's itchy and I'm sweating *so much*.

Maybe I'll need some Lynx Africa soon.

I really don't want to be here. Not today. Could I have just one more day before I have to say goodbye?

The church feels huge, like it's looming over me, and through the gentle tapping of the rain, dappled sunlight is streaming in through the stained-glass windows, lighting up the church. It's so beautiful. I can see tiny particles of dust swirling and drifting in the light, and everything seems to have slowed down.

Nan's casket is in front of me, but I don't look.

Somewhere in the crowd, Mum is watching me. *Mum.* But I can't think about that now either.

So, I look forward and begin to read my poem:

The Forest of Memories

There's a forest I know, just around the corner, one
dream away, tucked safely out of sight.

It's an enchanted, magical place
where everything slows down.

In springtime the bluebells sway in the cool breeze,
and in summer the sun shines bright.

In autumn the stream glistens and babbles. It
will tell you its secrets if you listen closely enough.

In winter ice sparkles and glitters and it
seems like all the world has gone to sleep.

But no: the forest is remembering.

Because this is the Forest of Memories,
and it's where I go to remember you.

I wander in, and find the day we sat in your tiny garden, eating cheese sandwiches and chocolate from the fridge. The sky was blue and blackbirds sung. I continue walking, and the leaves dance in the breeze. It reminds me of all the times we danced and laughed together in the kitchen. Seeing you dance SO BADLY to Mariah's "Honey" was one of the funniest moments in my life!

There's a quiet spot where I sit on an ancient fallen tree trunk. The rings on the tree and its damp, damp bark are traces of time gone by, a collection of stories. Do you remember all the hours we spent talking about Granddad and looking through old photos of him? You met at a dance and he said your eyes sparkled. He was always such a charmer!

When the rain gathers and gently falls in the Forest of Memories, I think of when we got the bus into town and went shopping together. I felt so special! It rained then, too, and we got soaked! You swore so much! When we got home you wrapped me in a blanket and made me hot chocolate.

The chatty, excited river babbles and leaps through the
Forest of Memories, and I think of your laugh. So
wicked and mischievous. A real cackle! Once
you started, you couldn't stop, and ...

"Erm..."

"Excuse me ... erm..."

... everyone would join in too.

I look down. I've lost track of where I am, and I don't
know what I'm meant to say next. I scan over my
poem, my handwriting neat and perfect – because it
matters to me that Nan's poem looks beautiful – but
I can't remember what I just said.

In the Forest of Memories ... I ... erm ... I–

Where was I?
    The words seem to jumble and move around the
page, and I just stand there. Then I make the mistake
of looking out at everyone, casting my eyes around
the church, desperately hoping someone can help me.
    I see Ruth and Eliana, looking worried ... and I

see *Mum* clasping her hands tightly together on her lap. She looks good. She's tanned and golden, and her long blonde hair shimmers with summery movie-star highlights. *All the travelling and fancy hotels have obviously done her the world of good*, I think begrudgingly.

For a moment, all I can think about is holding her. But no.

I don't want her. She left us. I don't want her here.

And then I see, far at the back, sitting next to their parents, Harriet and Joel.

I gasp – I can't believe it! I can't believe they're here. After everything that's happened and everything we've been through, they're still here when I need them.

Harriet mouths one word to me, and it's "sorry". I look at her and smile and mouth back, "Me too."

Joel smiles at me as if to say, "Go on, you've got this" and scrunches up his nose in a cute way.

There's an excruciating silence, and I look at my shoes.

No, Joel, I have not got this.

I don't know what to say, and I want to run away, and I feel dizzy, but I need to read the poem. Maybe I should start it again? One more try? But I feel dizzy, so dizzy, and lost, and everything feels blurry and I feel dizzy and—

Suddenly Dad is at my side, and he is propping me up, his arm around me. He coughs, and while I hold on to him for support, he continues reading my poem, his voice steady and calm:

In the Forest of Memories, I speak to the trees,
and they whisper your words back to me, saying,
"You can only do your best, James" and "My
gorgeous Glitter Boy! How you sparkle and shine!"

The blanket of leaves and moss on the ground in
autumn is as soft as your pyjamas, the ones you wore
when we watched Midsomer Murders together on
Sunday evenings. You always said you could guess
who the murderer was, but you NEVER got it right!

In the Forest of Memories, the sunlight feels warm
on my skin, gentle and reassuring, just like when
you held me and hugged me and kissed me.
That's not something I can ever forget.

The Forest of Memories keeps you with me, always,
through winter, spring, summer and autumn.

You are safe here. You are with Granddad.

You are loved, and you are mine.

And as he finishes the final line, I see that Dad's eyes are blurry and wet, and my chest starts heaving up and down, up and down.

But before I can cry, Dad is leading me out of the church. My legs feel heavy, and he's practically dragging me, and I hear someone let out the most painful, agonized scream I've ever heard.

I realize it's me.

A few people stand up to help, but Dad waves them away, and I bury my face into his suit, and then we're out, out of the church and into the sunlight.

We sit down on a damp bench, and I put my head in my hands. Dad rubs my back and tells me to take deep breaths, but I'm in such a state I can't catch my breath, and I look up at him and say, "I'm sorry! I've ruined Nan's funeral! And my phone … I turned it off! That day, I was going to see her … but I didn't. And I didn't tell you about her falls, and her chest pain, and… She could have been in a care home; they would have taken care of her… It's all my fault!"

But Dad just wraps his big arm around my shoulders and says, "Don't be silly, mate. *None* of this is your fault, and you haven't ruined anything."

But I know I have. I've messed up Nan's funeral! What are people going to be thinking and saying about me now? Maybe they're all waiting for us to come back in?

So, I say, "It's OK, I'll be fine. Let's go back in, Dad," and I push him away – *I have to make this right, I have to* – but he holds me tighter.

"You're much more important to me," he whispers.

"What?" I ask. I've never heard him say something like that before.

"You're more important than a funeral, of course you are! And Nan, well, Nan would want me to look after you, wouldn't she? And she's not really there any more, mate. She's not really in the church. She's in your Forest of Memories now. Isn't that what your poem was about?"

And I can feel tears prick at my eyes again, because maybe Dad really does see me and understand me.

But then I hear a shuffle of feet and a cough, and I look up and see *Mum* there.

I feel like someone has thrown a bucket of freezing-cold water over me. I try to pull myself away

257

from Dad, squirming and wriggling uncomfortably. I don't want her to see me like this.

Dad stands up and says, "Not now, Isla. He's upset."

Mum looks at me desperately and says, "I just wanted to check on you, James. To have a word … in private."

Dad looks furious. I realize then that he's standing between me and Mum, like he's protecting me from her. He sighs. We wait.

"Are you going to be OK if I leave you, James?" Dad says eventually, glaring at Mum.

I nod and bite my lip.

"OK," Dad says, rubbing my back. "I'll pop back into the church and speak to the vicar quickly, but I'll be back."

Dad plants a kiss on the top of my head and then nods at Mum curtly. He walks back into the church, but I can see him looking back at me, worry etched on his face.

Mum walks over to me, and I can tell she's nervous.

"Hello, sweetheart," she says. "Is it OK if I sit down next to you?"

I shrug.

Do what you want, I think. *It's a free world.*

She sits down. She smells of coconut and tropical sunshine, and her large black sunglasses make her look like she's some kind of celebrity. It all seems a bit out of place. *She* seems out of place.

We wait and wait. There's no way I'm going to speak first. Not to her.

"I tried ringing you," Mum begins, "and texting. And I sent you some postcards. Did you get the postcards?"

"Yes," I mutter.

"That's good, I'm glad. I … erm…"

"You left me, Mum," I say, and I feel like there's something trapped in my chest.

"Oh, darling, I'm so sorry. I didn't want to leave you. I really didn't. But I just couldn't stay in that house any more. I felt … I felt suffocated and so lonely. And I just wanted more…"

"I'm sorry I wasn't enough," I snap, folding my arms across my chest.

"Not you, never you," Mum continues. She sounds frantic now. "Your father and I had been having problems for such a long time, and we were arguing about everything. The bills, Nan, us, you … everything. And I got this job offer, and it seemed like everything I'd ever wanted. Travel and glamour and excitement, and I just couldn't say no."

"Then why didn't you take me with you?" I ask, and I realize I sound pitiful.

"Oh, James, I would have loved that! I wanted you to come, but it's not practical. I'm here, there and everywhere, and there'd be no stability for you. So, we decided I'd leave and you'd stay here."

"Thanks, thanks a lot," I say. "It's been AMAZING here without you, can't you tell? Such a good decision! I'm SO grateful."

"Please, James. I know I've got so much making up to do. I know. But if I'd stayed I would have been miserable, and you know I was always a rubbish mum, so flaky and irresponsible! Your dad was always the responsible one, so lovely with you."

Silence. I try and weigh it all up.

I don't know why, but I find myself thinking about Marsha P. Johnson, and a word that kept coming up about her: "kindness". Apparently she would give people parts of her outfit – beautiful scarves, jewellery, flowers from her crowns. It's like she was planting little seeds of kindness that would one day grow and thrive. This despite everything – despite all the terrible things life threw at her.

That's the kind of person I want to be someday.

Maybe, I think, *it's kindness that makes you strong?*

So, I take a deep breath and whisper, "You weren't a rubbish mum."

I see her blink a few times behind her sunglasses, and she takes my hand gently.

"Turns out all the glamour and travelling isn't that much fun without you. You were always my little star, weren't you? Always dancing and laughing and creating and dreaming and making everything so exciting!"

Was I? That all seems like such a long time ago now.

"And I miss that. I miss you," Mum continues shakily.

So, what do I do with all of this?

"Look, I'm away for a few weeks with work, but I thought…" Mum pauses. "I hoped that when I'm back we could go for dinner? And in the holidays I thought you might like to do some travelling with me, or…"

"I don't know about … erm, travelling with you… Dad needs me. I need to be here right now."

"Oh," Mum says, and she sounds crushed. "That's OK, I understand."

So, where do we go from here? What do I say? What kind of person do I want to be?

I take a deep breath.

"But dinner sounds OK," I say, looking up at her for the first time. "If you pay," I say, with a short laugh, "and there's pizza and cake and ice cream."

She laughs too, and then says, "It's a deal."

We sit in the church grounds together, and I close my eyes and let the autumn sunlight warm my face, just like in the woods. The rain has finally stopped. I can hear birds chirping, and everything else seems so far away. Mum places her hand in mine, and the two of us sit there, together again after what seems like such a long, long time apart.

CHAPTER 29

"How's it all going, lads? Everything OK in here, chaps? Need anything?"

"Erm, no thanks, Dad. We're STILL OK," I reply, blushing. Why does he have to be so embarrassing?

It's Sunday afternoon and Joel and I are sitting uncomfortably on the bed in my room.

Dad and I came home after the funeral yesterday and we both slept on the sofa for the afternoon. Then I woke up feeling energized, raring to go, like I *had* to do something. If I can face Mum, then I can do *anything*.

So, I asked him!

"Dad, erm… We've got this school project … you know, the one Joel and I are working on, and we haven'treallybeenspeakingmuch, and" – big, deep breath and gulp – "and we needtofinishhourproject, and I was hoping Joel could ... he could ... comeoversowecanworkonittogether?"

Dad raised his eyebrow and I felt sure, one hundred per cent, that he would say no, but he squared his shoulders like he was preparing for something big, something monumental, and said, a bit too loudly and enthusiastically, "OF COURSE! Of course, he can! Joel? Come round? YES! Absolutely!"

Maybe Dad just felt sorry for me after my emotional breakdown, my little diva fit, yesterday. Why else would he say yes?

So I texted Joel. Amazingly, he replied straight away.

Except, now that he's here, neither of us seems to know what to say and Dad is in my room *again*, shifting uncomfortably from one foot to the other and doing a lot of cool-dad finger-pointing and saying "mate" and "chaps" and "lads" a lot. He seems *incredibly* uncomfortable!

"I could do you some COOKIES?" Dad asks again.

"Dad, not to be rude, but your baking isn't ... erm... We're fine. We've just had a plate of biscuits, remember?"

Kindness, James!

264

"Oh, yep, lads! Of course, of course, chaps! I'll just be out in the garden, then. Let me know if you need any help…"

"Thanks, Dad," I say firmly.

When Dad's gone, Joel lets out a little laugh and nervously says, "I like your dad."

"He's all right," I say, rolling my eyes and laughing. And then I blurt out, "Look, I'm sorry. I'm really sorry! I shouldn't have pushed you or said what I said. I'm so ashamed of myself for shouting at you, and blaming you, and—"

"No, no!" Joel replies, wringing his hands together. "It's me who needs to apologize! I've spent a lot of time thinking about it all. And I feel terrible for lying to you about the WhatsApp group. I feel like all I ever do is lie to everyone at the moment."

I look at Joel and it only now occurs to me that he seems like he has the weight of the world on his shoulders – tired, upset, almost wounded. How can I fix this?

"It's all OK," I say. "I've been a complete jerk recently. I've been so wrapped up with Nan and everything that's been happening with Paul, and I just don't know how to deal with it or what to do… But I'm glad we're speaking again."

"Me too," Joel says, relaxing a little.

We sit for a while and Joel clears his throat a few times. Silence was fine in the woods, but here I can't cope with the not-talking. I jump up and I press play on Mariah's 1994 gospel-tinged hit "Anytime You Need a Friend", except it's the C&C Club Mix and it's ten minutes of pure joy.

Joel stands up and starts swaying to the music, backwards and forwards, his movements getting bigger and bigger and his hands held high above his head. He has his eyes closed and is miming along to the words, his mouth open wide – except he doesn't know the words and is just mouthing "rhubarbrhubarbrhubarbrhubarb" again and again. I laugh and start dancing too, and when the beat kicks in we start spinning around and around in circles. I've got my Mariah fingers moving across my face and fluttering up and down, pointing to the sky. We're swaying and laughing and then Joel's performing the song to me, gesturing wildly.

As the song comes to an end, we collapse on to the bedroom floor, laughing and panting, out of breath.

After a while, Joel says, "Can I give you some advice?" He looks unsure.

"It's OK!" I laugh. "Don't worry! I'm not going to bite your head off. Go on."

"I think you should tell your dad about, you know, Paul and the WhatsApp group."

"That's just what Harriet said, and I will, just not yet. Is that OK? I'm still trying to get my head around it," I say.

We're lying side by side on the floor.

"Oh, good. Of course, do it when you're ready," Joel continues, "but I think your dad might surprise you; I think he will be cool about it. And no one would mind ... if ... you know ... you *were* gay."

My breath catches, and I want to immediately leap up and say, "But I'm not, I'm NOT!"

But something stops me this time.

I might be.

I think I am?

But then again, I might not be.

And I think that's OK too.

So, I just say, "Thanks, Joel."

Joel shuffles over on the carpet so he's lying closer to me. Both of us are staring up at the ceiling.

He says, and it's so quiet I almost miss it, "And you wouldn't care if I was ... you know... Would you?"

"Oh, god, NO! No way! It's fine with me. It WOULD

be fine with me, if you were … you know…" I say.

This is all getting strange, so I sit up, running my fingers through my hair. The hair at the front is stuck to my forehead, sweaty and slick after all the dancing.

"We should probably get on with our project…" I say at EXACTLY the same time Joel sits up and says, "I want to tell you something…"

We laugh bashfully and I look at Joel, but the moment seems to have passed.

"Anyway, yeah, you're right, so much to do! I can't believe the presentation is on Thursday!" Joel says, but he looks disappointed. He studies the page in front of him for a minute, before adding, "And I really am sorry about not telling you about Paul and the WhatsApp group and what he was saying…"

"It's OK, honestly," I say, shaking my head, because the truth is I don't want to talk about it any more, and I don't want to tell Dad yet, and I don't want to ruin this afternoon with Joel by thinking about Paul.

But then I hear Dad's voice at the doorway:

"What's this about a WhatsApp group and Paul?"

OH.

NO.

CHAPTER 30

"I said, what's this about a WhatsApp group and Paul?" says Dad again, filling the doorframe. He's raising his eyebrow and tilting his head to one side.

"Nothing, Mr Turner," splutters Joel.

"It's nothing, Dad!"

It feels just like the time I was caught stealing from the sweet cupboard downstairs. I mean, what kind of dad has a cupboard full of sweets and chocolates and doesn't expect their kid to pinch a few now and again? OK, so I was in the process of taking *loads*, and I was going to hide them under my bed for a midnight feast with Mariah. I was so much younger then, like nine or something, but I still remember the feeling of guilt and shame and fear.

"Lads," Dad says as he steps into the room, "what

is this about Paul and a WhatsApp group? I know he can be a little … pain in the backside…"

He does? How?

Joel looks at me and I look at Joel, our eyes widening in fear, flashing back and forth. It would be comical if my heart wasn't beating ferociously in my chest and I wasn't so desperate to keep this from Dad.

He's going to hate me, and he'll be so let down and ashamed of me.

But then Dad says, "James," and he kneels down next to me, "if something is happening that's upsetting you, I'd really like to know. Please."

He looks so desperate to make things right between us.

I look at Joel, and he nods at me, and I feel like with him by my side…? I take a deep breath and finally decide to trust my dad.

"Well … Paul has set up a WhatsApp group with some of the boys at school … and…"

This is it. There's no going back.

"And he's saying that I'm gay." I flinch at saying *that word* out loud, but I carry on: "And he's saying that if anyone speaks to me, then … then … they're gay too… So, Nathan and Jake and lots of the other boys aren't talking to me…"

I can't look at Dad.

I realize I'm closing my eyes and I'm holding my breath.

"And Paul keeps following me around and whispering my name and kicking the back of my feet ... and I'm ... I'm scared, Dad."

I only look up when I feel his hand on my leg.

His face is close to mine, and for a moment I'm frightened he might hit me or tell me to leave the house, because that does happen to some kids, I know it does.

So, I wait. Dad seems to be wrestling with something, and his eyes are darting around the room. There's fury in them, but also some kind of sadness and grief.

Finally he says, "Thanks for telling me, James... Why didn't you tell me sooner?" I go to answer, but he seems to be speaking to himself and carries on saying, "Of course, you couldn't tell me because I've been a complete fool so why would you?"

Dad's face darkens.

He stands up and starts pacing up and down my room, my Mariah Carey posters tracking his every agitated move. He's muttering and talking to himself.

"That kid … that little… No, this isn't good enough… I'm going to… I'm going to…"

And he suddenly swoops out of the room!

I shoot up and scream, "DAD!", but he's gone.

I hear the front door slamming behind him.

Joel and I race down the stairs after him, our feet barely touching the ground. We throw our shoes on and dash outside. I can see him marching away in the distance and I know, I just *know* where he's going.

Joel and I run after him.

I am freaking out because I've never seen him this angry before. It reminds me of Harriet.

We finally catch up with him, and I'm panting as I grab his hand and he spins round. "Dad, please, please, don't! Just leave it," I beg.

"Not this time, James, no, sorry," he replies, and he shakes me off and continues charging forward. Joel and I scurry after him, and we're soon taking a left, and before I know it Dad is hammering on a front door, and I know who's going to answer it.

A man wearing a black T-shirt and very short shorts – *too short really, gross!* – answers the door. His face initially lights up in recognition and he opens his arms out in welcome, but then he must see Dad's snorting, glaring face. He stops and says, "Whoa! Hi, Dean! Boys! How's it going? Is everything OK?"

"Go and get your son," Dad says, his fists clenched at his sides.

"Dean, are you all right, mate? What's all this about?"

"I said, go and get him, now, Andy."

Andy looks cross and confused but calls upstairs, "Paul! Get down here now!"

A familiar whiny voice replies after a few seconds, "But, Dad, I'm playing on my Xbox!"

"NOW!" bellows Andy, and both men stand there in silence, staring at each other, like they're about to duel. Joel and I are standing either side of Dad and neither of us can breathe or speak or move.

And then I hear footsteps crashing and banging down the stairs and I see him.

"Dad, I said I was—"

Then Paul sees us and he stops. The colour drains from his face; all the bluster and bravado have gone and he's just a little, scared boy shuffling from one foot to the other at the bottom of the stairs.

"Is ANYONE going to tell me what's going on?" Andy asks, looking completely exasperated.

"Are you going to tell him, or am I?" Dad says

through gritted teeth. He never takes his eyes off Paul.

"It's nothing, just a bit of fun," mumbles Paul.

In one giant step my dad almost blocks the front door and Andy takes a step back.

"You think setting up a WhatsApp group so you and your little mates can bully my son is just a bit of fun, do you? DO YOU?"

I hold my breath. I'd give anything for the world to swallow me up right now. Surely this will only make things worse?

"Paul?" says Andy. "Paul? This better be a joke. Give me your phone. Now."

"But Daaadddddd!" Paul whines, and it makes me angry and I don't know why. It's like he thinks he can whine and moan and just wriggle out of it, like the slippery weasel he is, that everything will be forgotten and forgiven.

"I said, give me your phone NOW!" roars Andy, and Paul smacks his phone into his father's hand, defeated.

Andy puts on his glasses, so they're teetering on the end of his nose, and taps and taps at the phone. He mutters something under his breath and then turns to Paul and snaps, "Well, open it for me, then!

And get this chat group thing up so I can read it."

"Dad, it's private…" Paul begins, looking at me desperately, like I'm going to save him. Ha!

Andy gives Paul the scariest don't-mess-with-me face I've ever seen, and with a few jabs at the phone, Paul passes it back to him.

His dad scrolls through the phone, his eyebrows screwed up at first. But then his eyes widen and he begins shaking his head.

"You wrote all this?" he asks Paul.

Paul says nothing, just folds his arms and looks at the floor.

Andy keeps scrolling through Paul's phone, and I wonder what he must be thinking. Finally, he stops and rests his head in his hand, the bridge of his nose between his thumb and forefinger.

"This language is appalling, Paul," he says. "What have you got to say for yourself?"

"I was just mucking about! Wasn't I, James? Tell them!"

Before I can answer, Dad says, "Don't you dare speak to my son. Not now. Not ever again."

"Is this really what you think about gay people?" Andy asks, staring at Paul.

"Other kids were saying some stuff too!" Paul snaps.

"Hardly! And besides, I don't care about other kids! I care about what *you're* saying!" Andy growls. For a moment he looks too disgusted to speak. Then he says, "These words, this hatred, it's … it's horrible! Why would you care if James is gay or not? What's it got to do with you?"

Oh, no – now it's really *about me. Will they ask if I am…?*

But Paul just looks at the floor.

And then, almost as if in slow motion, Andy drops the phone on the floor. Paul screams as his dad lifts his foot and stamps down on the phone. He grinds his foot into the shattered, cracked phone and stamps on it again and again.

"Dad, that's my phone!" yells Paul, and he *still* doesn't seem to get it. He doesn't get what he's done.

"Get upstairs now! You can forget having a phone and you can forget that Xbox of yours. I'm so angry with you. Upstairs, NOW!"

And it's almost funny seeing Paul scuttle and whimper away.

Andy steps forward and Dad takes a step back, out of their hallway entrance, and in front of me, with his arm guarding me.

"James, I am so sorry about Paul. We didn't bring him up like this… He's been struggling lately, since… But there's no excuse for this. There will be consequences, I promise."

I nod, but I can't speak.

Dad says, "Just keep him away from my son, do you understand, Andy?"

Paul's dad nods grimly.

"If it happens again…" Dad begins, but I'm glad he doesn't finish his sentence.

Without saying another word, Dad turns and walks away, and Joel and I follow after him, trotting a few paces behind.

Joel mouths, "Whoa!" and I shake my head in disbelief.

But it's not over yet, surely? It can't be that easy, can it?

What if Dad is just standing up for me because he doesn't want anyone thinking I *might* be gay? And then what would happen if I *am* gay? Would he still have my back then? Would he still be there for me? Would he still go on a terrifying rampage and battle anyone who bullies me?

When we get home, Dad says, "So, Joel … erm … it's getting late. Fancy a pizza, boys? We can grab a pizza … ahem… Yep, I'll just ring your mum, Joel…"

Joel grins at me and shrugs, and we follow Dad into the living room, where Dad nods at me and turns on the TV.

And as Joel and I sit next to each other on the sofa, I have so many questions spinning and whirring around my head, and we should really practise for our presentation on Thursday. Instead, we just spend the evening watching *Jurassic Park* and eating pizza in silence. Every now and again, Joel catches my eye and mouths, "Whoa!" and I look at Dad and wonder what he's thinking.

CHAPTER 31

"Welcome, everyone, to our presentation! Today, Joel and I will be talking about…"

Joel looks at me encouragingly. We've rehearsed all week in our English lessons. In fact, we've rehearsed so much I *should* remember the next part… But now it's Thursday and I'm standing up in front of the class, speaking. Does my voice sound low enough? Is it manly enough? *Try not to gesticulate too much, James!* Keep your voice emotionless. Don't look at Paul. Paul who hasn't spoken to you all week. Paul who seems to be a simmering cloud of resentment. Paul who—

What am I meant to be talking about again?

My throat feels dry and scratchy, and I can see Paul smirking like a movie villain. After everything, he's still sneering at me! Maybe he'll never change.

Kindness makes you strong.

Joel nudges me.

"Oh yes!" I squeak. "We're going to be talking about an inspirational person from the LGBTQ+ community."

Phew, got there. Come on, James, pull it together! You've got this.

"Does anyone know" – Joel looks at Mr Hamilton, because we are *engaging our audience*, you see – "what the letters stand for in LGBTQ+?"

Harriet's hand shoots up. She waves it frantically backwards and forwards and side to side.

"Anyone apart from Harriet," Joel says, and I'm glad Harriet's perked up after her car crash of a presentation with Nathan, in which they both mumbled and definitely *did not* maintain eye contact with their audience.

"Anyone? Anyone know what they stand for?" Joel repeats, and I feel like I'm dying inside. If they know, they're not saying anything. Not a word. The water from the classroom sink seems to drip-drip really loudly.

Mr Hamilton puts his hand up, and the class giggle.

"Yes, Hamilton … *Mr* Hamilton…" I croak.

"Lesbian, gay, bisexual, transgender and queer or questioning," says Mr Hamilton, and Jake and Paul roll their eyes at each other.

Mr Hamilton scowls at them and continues, "The 'plus' sign also includes people who are non-binary or asexual. It could also include the pansexual, intersex, or gender-fluid communities."

Some children look confused, and Harriet says loudly, "I knew that!" and beams at everyone around her.

"Thank you, Mr Hamilton," says Joel. "That's correct, as you can see on... James ... *James!* The first slide, please?"

Yes! I can do that! I click on the whiteboard and our first slide whizzes up. We've used animated transitions, so the words all spiral and turn into place, *and* we've used a fancy Comic Sans font, so it looks epic!

And then I don't know what comes over me. Maybe it's Paul's ridiculous leering face and the realization that nothing I can do will ever be enough for him. Maybe it's because I'm nervous and I can't stop myself from speaking, or maybe it's because Mr Hamilton's rapt attention seems to have given me a bit of courage. Maybe, just maybe, some of my glitter and spark is coming back.

I say, "Erm … Mariah Carey also said that the letters stand for legendary, gorgeous, beautiful, tantalizing and quality, which does actually describe the person we're talking about today."

I wink, and the whole class laughs. *They're warming up!*

Apart from Paul, Jake and Nathan that is.

Joel adds, "We also have a handout and glossary of some other terms you might not know, which we will give out at the end."

I take a deep breath and say in a more serious tone, "We're going to talk now about someone from the LGBTQ+ community who has helped change the world and fought against people being bullied and treated badly."

"That person is Marsha P. Johnson," Joel says. "Marsha was a trans woman—"

"Well," I interject, "we're still not sure we've got that right. Some websites we looked at say that Marsha was a drag artist and some say Marsha was an African-American gay man. Some say she was a transgender woman and some say she was gender-nonconforming, and some say she was all of these things! So … erm … it just goes to show that we can never just assume how people identify, and we should listen to them when they tell us who they are." I blush. "Erm … sorry, carry on, Joel!"

Joel smiles at me and continues. "Marsha P. Johnson was also an activist who fought for gay rights and liberation. There was a bar in America called the Stonewall Inn, and the police arrested and beat up lots of gay people there. When this happened in 1969, being gay was classed as a mental illness, and people in the LGBTQ+ community were treated horrendously."

Joel says his words loudly and clearly, looking pointedly at Paul, who begins to squirm in his seat. As the presentation continues, I feel more and more confident.

A spark. A glimmer returning.

Joel continues talking about Marsha and her life. Soon, it's my turn again and I say, "Marsha P. Johnson stood up to the police and, along with her friend Sylvia Rivera, started lots of protests and riots, and is a very important figure when we talk about gay rights. Marsha and Sylvia looked after many of the Black and Latino LGBTQ+ community and lots of young people who were scared and had nowhere to go. Then, sadly, Marsha's body was found floating in the Hudson River in 1992."

Joel says, "We still don't know if she was murdered and what really happened to her."

Some kids gasp at this last sentence.

Harriet is grinning from ear to ear like a mischievous Cheshire Cat, and claps silently when I catch her eye.

After the whispers have died down, I add: "So that's why Marsha P. Johnson is an important person in history. She was brave, caring and courageous, and stood up for what was right. She believed in treating people with kindness. I think she taught us that we all have a voice and can change the world."

And then here comes the *amazing* bit: Joel suggested we play a Mariah Carey song while we conclude our presentation! I chose it, and it's a song called "I Am Free". Now, hear me out, it's not one of Mariah's better-known songs, like "Hero" or "Fantasy" or "Honey", but our presentation *is* about educating everyone. And that means educating people about Mariah, too!

In the song, Mariah sings about being a prisoner and how she was lost and lonely, but now she's free to live her life because of someone's love and kindness and acceptance. I feel like that's the whole point of what we've been talking about today.

And I don't know what happens to me, but I say, *completely unscripted*, "There are two women called Ruth and Eliana who live where my nan lives – *lived* – and they love each other. Whenever I see them, they are holding hands because, well, why shouldn't they? But some people said horrible things to them, and they don't hold hands any more..." I take a deep breath. "They shouldn't ever feel worried or scared to hold hands. We all have to be better and make sure everyone in our world feels safe and wanted and loved. And ... erm ... that's all I wanted to say."

As the music reaches its crescendo, and Mariah's really going for it, we show our final slides, which have pictures of LGBTQ+ icons and some information about their achievements: *Gwen Lally, Josephine Baker, Gladys Bentley, Edith Windsor, Elton John, Justin Fashanu, Lady Phyll, Billy Porter, Juno Dawson, Sam Smith, Ryan O'Connell, Lena Waithe, Laverne Cox, Rosie Jones, Darren Hayes, Carson Tueller* and *Michaela Jaé Rodriguez*.

They are all catalysts of change who have made, and continue to make, the LGBTQ+ community a richer, more accepting place.

The very last slide we show is a photograph of

Marsha – magnificent, charming, effervescent Marsha – beaming at the camera with a crown of beautiful flowers in her hair.

The music ends and we stand in front of the class, waiting.

I hold my breath.

Suddenly, Harriet jumps to her feet and starts clapping and the room *explodes*. Everyone starts to cheer and clap too. Rafe and Ameera do a celebration dance. Mr Hamilton mouths, "Well done."

I notice that Paul, Jake and Nathan have their arms folded and are looking at the floor. But none of that matters.

Other people's whispers and jabs and pokes and jeers and nastiness should never make us feel like we are not worthy of happiness.

I smile at Joel. It's been a long time since I've felt *accepted* in class, and I can't help but feel a bit hopeful.

CHAPTER 32

The first part of lunch goes by quickly. Rafe bounces by and gives us a thumbs up, saying, "Well done! That was really cool!"

I consider ignoring him, because that's what *he's* done to *me*, but there's something in his eyes, something apologetic, that makes me rethink. So, I smile and say, "Thanks, Rafe."

Kindness, James!

Anna stops by for a chat and tells us about her uncles. It's lovely to see her so animated and happy, and Joel seems to light up listening to her stories about them.

We spend the rest of lunch in the playground watching Harriet and Ameera rehearse a new dance that is proving *very* difficult. I stand to the side and bop along and eventually join in with the dance, as subtly and quietly as I can.

A spark. A glimmer returning.

Paul seems annoyed by this, though. I can see him whispering about me with Jake and Nathan, and every now and again he points at me and laughs and minces around the playground, swishing his hair, with his hands on his hips.

Four days. He's managed to leave me alone – more or less – for four days even after the WhatsApp thing and his dad's threats hanging over him.

"What a cretin," Joel says, shaking his head and laughing dismissively.

I try not to look and just focus on Ameera and Harriet.

"James!" Mrs Gallagher calls from across the playground.

Uh-oh! I've been avoiding her. Every choir rehearsal she's asked about my permission slip, and every time I've told her my dad has *definitely* signed it and I can *definitely* go, BUT I forgot it and left it at home. I even tried – which was pretty sneaky of me – telling her I've already given it to her, and she must have lost it. But she just said, "That's OK, James. I've got some spare copies in my desk… Here you go… Just bring it in tomorrow…"

Foiled again!

So, when she calls across the playground, I look for somewhere to hide, then pretend I'm busy playing, then pretend I can't hear her … but Mrs Gallagher soon catches up to me.

"Hi, James! I just wondered if you've got your permission slip? It would be such a shame to miss" – she lowers her voice and looks around her like she's on a covert, secret operation – "to miss Mr Hamilton's wedding surprise."

"Oh, YES! I had it in my bag this morning, and, erm … well … I took it out and this, like, MASSIVE – and I mean HUGE – gust of wind came along and BLEW it out of my hand!" I say. I feel like I should win an Oscar for that performance. (Just like Mariah should have won an Oscar for her role in *Glitter*. Robbed, I tell you!)

I grin broadly at Mrs Gallagher, but she doesn't look convinced. "Oh dear," she says – and she's smart, there's no getting round her, "I can just ring your dad, if you want? His verbal permission would be fine?"

Could I answer the phone when she rings and pretend to be Dad? Mimic his voice? *GGRRRRR!*

Probably not.

"Shall I give him a ring then, James?"

"NOOOOO! No! I mean, no thanks, Mrs Gallagher. He's not very well at the moment. Lost his voice. So, I'll just get the slip to you tomorrow..." I say.

"OK, James. Tomorrow really is the last day. I don't want you to miss singing at the wedding because you've worked so hard, and I know how excited you are about it. I really hope you can come," Mrs Gallagher says, and I feel bad for lying to her.

When she leaves, Joel says, "Isn't everything fine now with your dad? Just ask him!"

But Dad and I have formed a fragile understanding since Sunday, and I don't want to upset him. We talk about the garden, and Auntie Kathy and Weird Bruce, and maths, and homework, and films. Dad occasionally asks if school is OK, and I know what he means, and I know he wants to hear that everything's fine now. He's only just let me have Joel round, and I feel like I can't ask for something more, not yet.

So, we don't talk about Paul. Or Joel. Or Mariah. Or Mum. Or Nan.

It's tedious, but safe.

Mr Hamilton's wedding and the permission slip might just change all that.

So, I just say to Joel, "Yeah, I will. I'll ask him tonight. It'll be fine!"

But the truth is, I don't know if it will be.

"That was such a GAY presentation! I can't believe those two!" Paul says loudly, making sure Joel and I can hear.

We're standing outside class, lining up after lunch and waiting for Mr Hamilton. Paul seems unable to control himself.

Jake and Nathan are with him, and they look at me quickly, uncomfortable and guilty, and then turn back. Nathan laughs nervously and says, "Yeah ... well gay..."

And then it's as if everything stops. I turn around ... *and Mr Hamilton is there.*

"Get inside now, everyone," he says. His voice is barely a whisper, and it sounds cold and menacing. "Inside *now*."

He's glaring at Paul, Jake and Nathan. We begin to file into class. Paul looks at the ground, and I bite my lip.

Here we go.

We sit down and Mr Hamilton stands at the front of the class. Some children at the back of the line obviously haven't seen or heard the exchange, and Rafe and Ameera come into class laughing and talking.

"NOT a word. Not one word from anyone. Sit down in SILENCE." Mr Hamilton's voice is full of fury.

Rafe and Ameera immediately sit down, looking around them in confusion.

Mr Hamilton has never spoken to us like this before. In fact, he's hardly ever raised his voice, because we just *know* how far we can push it with him. He's strict – very strict – but he lets us have a laugh and a joke every now and then.

And then Mr Hamilton's shoulders slump and he looks defeated. All his rage seems to seep away from him.

He turns his back to us and begins writing on the board.

Maybe he won't say anything?

But, midway, he stops. He turns back around to face us.

We are silent. My chest hurts.

"I was… I heard something outside our classroom right now, and it's made me really cross. But then I thought… Well, I wasn't going to say anything, I was going to let it slide. But I just can't."

I think he might have something in his eyes because he wipes them quickly. I feel my face burning. I just want him to ignore it all. I felt so happy after our presentation; let's just go back to that. Let me get on with it, let me deal with it. Please.

But I know, deep down, I can't deal with this on my own.

"I've just heard some pupils in our class describing one of the presentations this morning as 'gay'. Now from the tone of the comment, I presume they meant it's 'rubbish' or 'uncool'?"

There are a few nervous giggles, but the kids soon stop when Mr Hamilton looks in their direction.

"Is this the first time 'gay' has been used like that here?"

Silence.

"How long have members of our class been using the word 'gay' like this?"

No one moves, no one speaks.

"I SAID, HOW LONG HAS THIS BEEN GOING ON FOR?"

Mr Hamilton's voice is a bellow, a roar. I see Joel and Nathan jump and flinch, and some children gasp. He's never shouted at us like this. Slowly, Harriet raises her hand.

Please, please put it down, I think. *Please. Just this once.*

"Thank you, Harriet." Mr Hamilton nods at her.

"It's been going on all term. It's not everyone, but a lot of people in our class have been saying it. And some boys have been calling other kids gay, too, like it's the worst thing in the world. Which it totally is not!"

Mr Hamilton takes a shaky breath. "All term? SIX WEEKS? And no one, NO ONE, thought to come and speak to me? I can't believe members of our class have been doing this. I'm gay. Sam is bisexual. Is that a problem? Is it? What's the point in doing all this work about respecting other people if you behave like THIS? I am SO … *disappointed*."

I can feel my hands start shaking. I don't like it when people shout, and I feel like everyone is looking at me. This is all about *me*. I can feel tears pricking at my eyes but I push them down. I will not cry. I will NOT cry. Instead, I look at the floor.

Mr Hamilton continues, and his voice seems steadier now: "It was tough back in my day. When I was at school everything was 'gay'. That pencil's so 'gay'. A missed penalty in a football game was 'gay'. Anyone they thought was rubbish, or quiet, or shy, or didn't fit in was 'gay'. Gay, gay, gay. I heard it everywhere I went. Can you imagine how terrifying it is to be young and confused about whether you're gay or not, and to keep hearing that word being used to belittle others? It made me feel scared, and it made me afraid of being gay, even admitting it to myself."

He wipes a tear from his eye and suddenly seems to be talking to me, just me, even though he's looking ahead.

"And what happens if we have students in our class – OUR class, which is meant to be a safe and accepting place – what happens if we have students who might be confused about their sexuality, or who might be gay or lesbian or bisexual or transgender? How do we make them feel when we use words so carelessly? They're going to think that they're rubbish, or not enough, because they've been hearing some of you flinging around that word like that all term. ALL TERM!"

Joel turns round to look at me.

I look back at him, and something shifts inside me.

Mariah Carey.

Marsha P. Johnson.

Dad.

Nan.

Harriet.

Mr Hamilton.

Joel.

I find myself standing up. I am standing up. Yep, that's me. Just standing up in class.

"Yes, James?"

"I feel… I feel…" My voice is shaking. "I think a lot of us feel bad because we didn't say anything. Me and Joel, we've even done our project on it, but … there's been – and I'm not mentioning any names here – there's been kids saying everything's 'gay' for ages, and kids bullying other kids and calling them 'gay'. I think we should have all said something or told them to stop."

I sit down, shaking. What is going on with me?

A spark. A glimmer returning.

Mr Hamilton sits down. He seems to have not heard what I said. He just sits, staring at the classroom floor.

No one speaks or moves.

My skin is itchy, and I immediately regret standing up and speaking. I want Nan to just come and take me away from this classroom right now, and I want to curl up under a duvet.

The silence and stillness seem to stretch on for

ages. Then Mr Hamilton looks up at us all and says, his voice wobbling, "Rafe, would you mind just popping out and getting Mrs Garcia for me, please?"

Rafe nods and scurries out of the classroom. We sit and wait.

It feels like for ever.

Finally, Mrs Garcia knocks at the door. She always knocks at our classroom door. I like her. She has lightly bronzed skin, and today she's wearing a fitted suit and a little jaunty, colourful neckerchief, a bit like an air hostess. Whenever she moves along the corridor you can hear her *way* before you see her because she clip-clops along in little high-heeled shoes and makes a point of saying hello to all the children and staff.

"Is everything OK, Mr Hamilton?" Mrs Garcia looks concerned.

"Erm … no. No, it's not. We've had some incidences of children in our class … in my class … describing things as 'gay' and calling other children 'gay' as if it's a bad thing, something to be ashamed of. And…"

Mrs Garcia steps into the classroom quickly. "Oh. Oh dear. That is such a shame. Mr Hamilton is always talking about this class and how proud he is of you. It's such a shame to hear this."

"And what makes me so sad," Mr Hamilton continues, "is that … is that…"

He bites his lip and looks away from us all. Mrs Garcia crosses the classroom quickly. She touches Mr Hamilton's hand gently, carefully, and then turns her back to us, to block him from our sight. Some of the kids look around at each other and begin to whisper.

But I don't.

I listen so carefully, so carefully to what they're saying.

"I've … I've … I've lost it, sorry. I don't know what's happened," Mr Hamilton is saying. I can see his shoulders shaking. "Will you … will you take over for me for a bit so I can get myself together, please?"

"Of course," Mrs Garcia whispers to him kindly.

He leaves the room, but before he does, he looks at me. His eyes are full of pain and guilt and something else.

And then he's gone.

"OK, 6H. Mr Hamilton has just gone to the toilet for a few minutes. I think we all need to have a long chat and a think about how we're going to deal with this because it's *not* how we behave in our school.

But it won't be now, because I think Mr Hamilton will want to be here for that. Is that OK?"

We nod.

"Right, then. Is it science this afternoon? Now, do you normally hand out the science books, or do you have them in your drawers?"

And just like that, the class breathes a collective sigh of relief. Harriet squeezes my hand under the table.

But I don't feel like I can move.

CHAPTER 33

Mr Hamilton doesn't come back for the rest of the afternoon.

Mrs Garcia says she's *not* going to get out the empty bottles, red food colouring, mini marshmallows and Cheerios that Mr Hamilton had brought in for our science lesson. We were supposed to be mixing them all together to represent the make-up of blood. Instead, she quickly finds some videos on the internet, and we spend the afternoon researching, writing and drawing diagrams all about our blood and the role it plays in our bodies.

I think we're all glad of the quiet and calm, and I try hard to focus on my work. I can feel Paul's gaze from across the room, and my neck and shoulders ache from staring down and absolutely *not* turning around.

At the end of the day, Joel, Harriet and I walk home, and we're all quiet and subdued. No one wants to talk about Mr Hamilton and what happened today.

It's amazing how quickly everything changes, isn't it? This morning I thought our presentation had made a difference and changed everyone's minds. I even thought for a minute that Joel and I could be trailblazers too, and be as brave and resilient and cool as the people we talked about.

Was that stupid? For people like Paul, it doesn't matter what you say to them; they will always cling to their hatred and use everything you say and do against you.

I wonder if there's any point in constantly explaining and justifying to some people why *everyone* deserves respect and has a right to be included. People who fight like this all their life – they must be tired, mustn't they?

I mean, I'm eleven, and I'm already fed up.

Later that evening, Dad and I are watching TV, but all I can think about is what happened today.

I hope Mr Hamilton's OK.

Mr Hamilton … wedding … permission slip!

I think about how I found a small glint of courage inside today to stand up and speak. How Mr Hamilton stood up today in front of the whole class and told us who he was, who he really was. Every day at school, every single moment, he's been there for me, trying to reach me to make sure I'm OK. And I want to say thank you. I want to be at his wedding so he knows how much he means to me, so he knows that he's changed my life.

I *have* to be at that wedding.

Besides, Dad will be fine with it! Didn't he let Joel come round on Sunday night?

Come on, James, be more Marsha P. Johnson, I tell myself.

So, I finally pluck up the courage to ask Dad one last time. As we eat dinner, I say "Yyuuummmmmm" and "This is *delicious*, Dad", even though it's pretty repellent. I tell him that the presentation went amazingly and nothing, absolutely *nothing* happened for the rest of the day. Then I help to wash and wipe up, and finally, just to seal the deal, I offer him a cup of tea and I even ask him how his day's gone.

I don't think he suspects *a thing*!

Obviously, the plan is that I will have buttered him

up so much and he'll be in such a good mood that he'll jump up and down and squeal, *Of COURSE you can sing at your teacher's wedding, my darling son!*

After dinner, I'm wrapped up in a blanket and lying curled up on the sofa with my feet on Dad's lap. He's sat with his arms folded, chuckling away at the TV.

"Daaaaadddddd…" I begin, hoping I sound sweet and innocent and oh-so-trustworthy.

"Ha!" Dad laughs, tickling my feet. "I *knew* you wanted something!"

"What?!" I splutter, trying my best to look offended. But he's joking, he's laughing, so is this going well?

"James, when you tell me my cooking is delicious, I know you're up to something. Come on, spit it out."

"Sooooooo," I begin, "you know I asked ages ago about singing at Mr Hamilton's wedding? Well, we have to bring in our permission slips tomorrow because it's on Saturday."

"Right, but I thought we'd already talked about this, mate?" Dad says, staring at the television.

"I was hoping… I *really* want to go with the choir, Dad. We've been rehearsing all term, and I really want to go."

"A teacher's private life should be private, that's all, sorry, son," says Dad.

"But why? Why won't you tell me *why*?"

"Look," says Dad, turning off the TV and then turning to face me, "I just think it's best you don't go. OK?"

"No, no, it's *not* OK! Why don't you want me to sing at his wedding? What's your problem with him?" I ask, digging my nails into my palms.

I want to hear him say it.

"I'm not thrilled as it is that Mr Hamilton is your teacher. Don't you think this whole" – he drops his voice to a whisper – "*gay thing* has got you in enough trouble as it is?" At least Dad looks ashamed of himself for saying it. But he carries on anyway, each word like a little stab in my chest: "I just think you're eleven and you don't need to be worrying about all this stuff and reading books about it and… You're too young."

"Dad," I say as patiently as I can, "you do know having a gay teacher, or even reading a book with a gay character in it, isn't going to suddenly make me gay, don't you?"

But it might make me feel less alone. It might help me make sense of everything.

"In Year 3 with Miss Davies," I continue, my voice

rising, "we learnt about the Tudors and Henry VIII, and I didn't put on a load of weight, get gout and go around marrying, divorcing and beheading all the girls in the playground, did I?"

Dad sighs. "Look, it's fine for Joel to come round every now and again. But just keep your head down for a bit, mate. You've had this whole thing with Paul, and you don't want to give him any more ammunition to use against you..."

I stare at Dad and try to work out what he's saying.

"Dad ... it's not *my* fault Paul has—"

"I know, I know," Dad interrupts. "I'm not saying it is. I just don't think it's appropriate to have a teacher forcing all this on ten-and eleven-year-olds."

"Mr Hamilton isn't forcing anything on me, Dad! He doesn't even *know* about the choir singing! It's a SURPRISE!"

I can feel that I'm almost shouting now, and I know I'm going to start struggling to get my point across soon because I'm confused and cross and I can't deny it any more. It's pretty obvious: my dad is homophobic. He only went over to Paul's because he felt my *reputation* had been damaged, like some poor Victorian woman whose status in society needed saving.

My dad just doesn't like gay people, and there's nothing I can do to change his mind.

"Look, James, I've got … erm … got no problem with people being … you know…"

No problem? NO PROBLEM?

"… but you're eleven, and I don't want you getting all confused…"

I want to shake him and say I'm *already* confused and hurt. I wonder if Dad knows how invisible I've felt for so long.

"… and I … I just don't think kids should be singing at their teachers' weddings."

Right. Like he'd stop me from singing at another teacher's wedding who *wasn't* gay.

What would happen if I told Dad I was gay, or bisexual like Sam? Would he still love me, and give me hugs and cuddles? Would he hate me, throw me out on to the street? Or would he tell me it's fine as long as I keep my head down?

"Look, James," Dad says sadly, interrupting my spiralling thoughts. "I'm doing my best here. I'm really, really trying since your mum left, and yeah, I don't know what I'm doing all the time, but this just doesn't feel right."

"But Dad—"

"No, that's it, sorry. End of conversation, mate. You're not going."

I can see from his resolute expression that there's no changing his mind.

And you know what? I give up. I tried.

So I just nod and say wearily, "OK, that's fine. I won't go."

I climb off the sofa and traipse upstairs, leaving Dad staring at the TV.

That's it, then.

No wedding for me.

CHAPTER 34

"So, how did it go with your dad?" Joel asks as we walk to school the next day. Harriet's walking a few paces in front of us with Rafe and some other kids. They're talking about Mr Hamilton's outburst yesterday and I hear Ohrim say, "I hope he's back today." So do I. It's a miserable grey day and I feel shivery and cold. I have my school coat on, and my hands are stuffed into the pockets.

"How did it go with Dad? Erm… Not great." I sigh. "He said no, so I'm not going to be able to go." I keep my voice flat.

"WHAT? Why? That's so rubbish!" says Joel.

"Yeah, it's rubbish," I say, avoiding the question.

"I thought he was getting his head around it all, and he stood up for you with Paul and his dad…?"

I shrug. "Apparently I'm too young for *gay stuff*."

We walk on in silence, all these questions swirling around in my mind. Eventually I say quietly, "Will you take some … some photos for me tomorrow? At the wedding?"

"Of course I will," Joel says. "But, well, you know, maybe your dad will change his mind?"

I smile at him and say, "Yeah, maybe," but I know there's just as much chance of Mariah Carey popping round ours for a cup of tea.

A spark. A glimmer.

Gone.

We wander into the school gates and around the playground, and soon the younger children start trickling in with their parents. I see a little girl in reception class holding her nan's hand and skipping into the playground, and I think I'd like to be back in reception and holding *my* nan's hand again. Everything was so much simpler then. I wonder what Nan would make of all of this, and then I have to look away.

"You OK?" Joel asks.

"Yeah, fine. I need to go and tell Mrs Gallagher I can't go to the wedding. I'll see you in class."

"See you," says Joel.

*

After my visit to Mrs Gallagher, I creep into Mr Hamilton's class just as everyone is sitting down, and I breathe a sigh of relief that I'm not too late; that would draw too much attention.

Mrs Gallagher was *not* happy when I told her, and I feel awful that I've let her down *the day before the wedding*. She offered to speak to Dad, but I told her there was no point, that we had made plans for the day, and it was my fault for not checking.

She didn't look convinced, but there was nothing she could do.

Mr Hamilton is back, thank goodness. He is sitting at his desk in the front, looking tired and pale, but he smiles at me as I take my seat.

There's a strange atmosphere in class today. Everyone's sitting with their arms folded, all their equipment out and ready to go, and we wait for Mr Hamilton to begin.

"OK, so I wanted to start today by saying that it's a new day. I also want to apologize for yesterday afternoon," Mr Hamilton says. "As you know, I'm not really one to shout, and I'm sorry if it frightened some of you…"

"It frightened me, it really did!" says Ameera, laughing.

We all laugh now, and it breaks some of the tension.

"I'll be the first one to admit that I don't think I handled things very well yesterday, at all," continues Mr Hamilton. "I really let it get to me, and hearing the word 'gay' used like that brought back a lot of difficult memories for me, so I'm sorry. And I'm sorry we missed out on our science experiment too."

He stands up and begins moving around the classroom.

"We do, however, need to address what has been happening in our class. There used to be a series of laws called Section 28 that prevented teachers from even talking about these things in school. Section 28 did a lot of damage. But it's gone now, so we can talk, and we must." He stands by the window, looking out into the playground. He looks haunted, like he's remembering something from long ago.

"So, let's start," he says, shaking his head. "When we bully someone because we think they're gay and don't deserve the same respect as everyone else, it's called – well, I wonder if anyone knows what it's called?"

Lots of children look at the floor, but Joel, brave Joel, puts his hand up and says, "It's called homophobic bullying, Mr Hamilton."

Mr Hamilton nods and says, "That's right. Now, we know that bullying of *any* kind is not allowed in our school, don't we? And I think we need to really consider, as a class, how we speak to one another."

Anna puts her hand up and says, "It's been making me feel really upset hearing some of our class call things 'gay' and tease other people because I have two uncles called Andrew and Jake, and they're together. It makes me feel like people are disrespecting them."

Mr Hamilton says, "What do you like doing with your uncles, Anna?"

"Well," she says, "I like it when they take me and my sister Coco out for a special day and we go to the cinema and get popcorn and sweets and then we go for lunch."

"That's really lovely, Anna, thanks for sharing."

Mr Hamilton turns to the rest of us and says, "You see, there are lots of different kinds of relationships, and most people are just trying to get on with their lives. It's tough enough out there without us adding more misery to it. Wouldn't you agree?"

Everyone except Paul and Jake and Nathan nods.

"And," Mr Hamilton continues, "you might think that it's just a joke, or it's only a word, but every time you use that word to describe someone or something as rubbish or uncool you are saying that being gay is all of those things too. That we are worthless. James and Joel taught us yesterday about the prejudice the LGBTQ+ community faces, and I will not accept that in our classroom."

At that moment, Mrs Garcia pops her head into our classroom and says, "I'm just checking how everyone is today, Mr Hamilton." She says it loudly and dramatically, like it's been scripted.

"Hello, Mrs Garcia," Mr Hamilton replies, "perfect timing, actually! Almost like we planned it!"

He winks at us, and we giggle. Obviously, they planned it. Teachers are sneaky like that.

"Indeed!" Mrs Garcia laughs. "Now, I've been talking to Mr Hamilton about yesterday, and I think he's started telling you about the consequences of using 'gay' in a pejorative – that means negative – manner and the consequences of *any* homophobic bullying in our school."

We all nod.

"That's perfect. We've also been talking about some improvements we can make to our school and curriculum. They won't happen straight away, but I want you all to know there will be some changes," says Mrs Garcia.

We all nod again.

"Great!" says Mrs Garcia. "Well, have a good day. I'll be out in the playground at lunch keeping an eye on everyone, and I'll pop in this afternoon to see how you're all getting on."

It feels good to know that Mrs Garcia is taking this seriously. I wonder what would have happened last year if Miss Wilson had listened to me.

Mr Hamilton gets out a big sheet of paper and lays it across one of the desks at the front. Some of the kids at the back stand up to get a better look.

"So, I'd like to create a class charter about being *allies* and how we're going to tackle homophobic bullying. Does anyone know what an *ally* is?"

Harriet waves her arm up and down.

"Is it something to do with lying?" Rafe says.

Harriet rolls her eyes at me.

"Good try. I can see how you got that, Rafe, but it's not, no," Mr Hamilton says. "Harriet?"

"It means supporting, listening and helping others," Harriet says confidently.

"Excellent, Harriet," Mr Hamilton says.

And then Harriet stands up, like she just can't control herself, and I die a little bit inside. *What is she doing?*

"I've been talking to my mum about it a lot, and she says it means finding out about other people's lives. I have to make sure – I mean, *we* have to make sure we don't treat people like victims."

"Thank you, Harriet," Mr Hamilton says, smiling and gesturing for her to sit down.

But Harriet ignores him and carries on: "Mum says I have to – I mean, *we* have to think about why some voices are heard and some aren't. But you can't just think you know better than other people and go racing in and beating people up. You have to listen to Ja— I mean, you have to listen to them…"

I giggle.

"Thank you, Har—" Mr Hamilton begins, but she keeps going.

"AND another thing. The LGBTQ+ community doesn't need our thoughts and prayers and sympathy. It needs our action!" Harriet raises her hand and pumps her fist in the air.

I grin up at her and start clapping really loudly. The rest of the class join in, and Rafe shouts out, "Well done, Harriet!"

"Yes, very well put, Harriet. Very … *stirring*," Mr Hamilton says, trying to keep a straight face as he quietens us down.

Harriet sits down and looks straight ahead, her face flushed. I take her hand under the desk and squeeze it tightly. *Brilliant, fierce Harriet.*

Soon, everyone starts talking, and the classroom is buzzing again with ideas. At the end of the session, we sign our names on the class charter. I use my soon-to-be-famous-Mariah-Carey-songwriter signature.

Paul reluctantly scribbles his name and then slams his pencil down afterwards.

It feels like we're agreeing to do better, to *be* better. It feels like we are a team once more.

When we're finished talking, Mr Hamilton says, "OK, so that was a bit of a longer session than planned, and I'm sure you'll be really sad to know we've missed maths…"

There are some cheers and Mr Hamilton grins.

"… but I think it was important for us to confront this as a class, and for you to know what we, as a school, are doing to tackle this. Right, you've been sat here for a long time. Let's go and have a run around outside, and if anyone needs to talk to me, or has any more ideas, come and see me."

Everyone gets up and begins pushing and racing outside, but Mr Hamilton doesn't tell anyone off. Before I leave the classroom, I stop in front of him.

"Thanks, Mr Hamilton," I say, and I have to bite my lip. "For everything."

I want to say so much more, but I'm at a loss for words.

I hope he knows how much he means to me.

"Any time, James," Mr Hamilton says, his eyes glistening.

CHAPTER 35

That night I listen to Mariah's 1999 *Rainbow* album. I've been playing "Can't Take That Away" again and again as I write a poem. The song is about not letting anyone tear you down and how we all have a light, a glimmer of hope, which shines inside of us, even in the darkest of times.

Mariah Carey, my *Elusive Chanteuse*: I'd like to say that *For the Record*, you are *My All*, you help me make it *Through the Rain* and even when *Angels Cry* and I want to hide away and *Camouflage* myself, I *Thank God I Found You*.

There's a knock on the door. I sigh. It will be Dad telling me to turn Mariah off, or telling me it's time for bed.

He peeks around the door and says, "All right, mate? All right if I … come in?"

I wonder why he's asking, because he never usually asks? "Erm … yeah … fine," I say, turning Mariah off and putting my notepad to one side.

He shuffles in and sits down next to me on my bed. "So, everything OK today, mate? Good day?"

"Yeah, fine," I say, not looking at him. Somehow, I think he won't want to hear about Mr Hamilton or about the talk we had in class.

"Good, good," Dad says, and he pats me on my knee.

We sit for a while, and I feel sad because I don't know what to say to him any more. So much of what I say and do only seems to make him cross and sigh and mutter.

He seems nervous and is fiddling and tapping his fingers a lot.

"You OK, Dad?"

"Yep, fine! I … I was sorting out Nan's room today, because you know we'll have to … er … sell the house soon, don't you?"

I know we have to, and it feels horrible to think about other people living in Nan's house. It feels wrong, strangers invading it and erasing the fact that she was ever there.

But I suppose it *might* be a young family with a cute baby and a tiny, fluffy dog, and they might make Nan's house feel alive again with dancing and singing and happiness. That would be nice. It shouldn't be left empty. She wouldn't want that.

Dad continues, "Well, while I was clearing out her bedroom, I found this." He rummages in his pocket and pulls out an envelope. "It was in your nan's special make-up and jewellery box. You know, the one that plays music? I ... erm ... I had to leave that until last because..."

Because it must have been so hard, I think. I remember that special box, sitting on her bedside table for all those years. There was never anything valuable in it, but I used to think it was full of the most beautiful, sparkling treasure. She'd let me wear her necklaces and rings while I performed and danced – and they'd make my fingers go green, but I loved it. She had little trinkets and gifts in there that Granddad had given her, and a black-and-white photo of them together at the beach. There was a little heart-shaped locket too, which had a faded picture of Dad in there taken just after he was born.

So, I know why he had to leave looking through Nan's special treasure box until the last moment. You can throw out and recycle most things, and give other things to charity shops; but some things, for whatever reason, are too special to part with. They hold too many memories. And I think Dad has been trying to avoid those memories ever since Nan died.

He hands me the envelope, and I gasp when I see that it has my name on it, written in Nan's swirling handwriting.

It's sealed.

"I saved all her ... erm ... everything she had in her special box," says Dad. "I thought you could have it?"

I hold on to the envelope and say, "Thanks, Dad. I'd like that."

He pats my knee again.

"I can leave you with the ... letter, if you want? To read? You probably don't want me here."

Dad gets up to go, but I don't want him to leave. Not for this.

If I want things to change, I have to change too.

"No, it's OK," I say. "We can ... we can read it together."

Dad sits down and coughs and then clears his throat. And then coughs again. And then once more. His fingers are tapping on his legs.

I slowly, slowly open the envelope, and I think I can smell Nan's perfume. I try to be careful; I don't want to rip or damage it.

I unfold the letter and hold it so that Dad can read it too.

To my darling James,

It feels strange to be writing you a letter — it's what we did in the old days, you see! But as I get older, I realize that our time doesn't last for ever, and there's so much I want to say. At least if it's written in a letter it will stay with you, tucked away safely in your heart, like you are tucked so lovingly in mine.

First of all, I want you to know that I love you very much. When your mum and dad brought you home from the hospital, I remember seeing you for the very first time. You were tiny! My little bobbin! I knew from that moment that I loved you completely.

There's something very special about a grandma's love for her grandchildren. I love your dad very much and always will — he's my son, even if he is stubborn and pig-headed sometimes!

322

But having a grandson like you has made me so happy. I feel a special love for you that I've never felt before. You make me see the world in a totally different way. I love your passion and enthusiasm, your energy and creativity. You write so beautifully and with such honesty. I've loved listening to Mariah Carey with you and sharing your passion for her music and lyrics. Don't feel bad that I'm such a better dancer than you, though, will you? Just remember how good I was at dancing to "Honey"!

I love how you always try your best, and how you always think of others. Just remember to think of yourself sometimes too.

I know you've been through so much, and I wish I could make it so that you never get hurt or upset or feel let down ever again. Every nan wants to do that for her grandchildren. But I can't. I've watched you recently and I can tell that some of your spark, your carefree happiness, has gone. I respect that you don't want to tell me why, but please remember that you must tell someone.

Someone, somewhere, will listen to you and be the support you need.

I was so angry and lost when your granddad died, and I kept it all bottled up for a long time. And that hurt. It hurt me, and it hurt your dad.

Speaking of your dad, go easy on him. You're more like each other than you could ever know, and he loves you so much. When we love someone that much, we want to keep them safe and protect them from everything — and because of that, we make mistakes. He has made mistakes. But you are everything to him.

I know how hard it is to talk about your mum, and I know you feel like she abandoned you. She made a decision, and, whilst I don't agree with it, it was her decision to make, and she will have to live with it for the rest of her life. She always was a dreamer, always wanted more, but I think she got a bit lost along the way, a bit swept up in it all. I know she loves you, though, and I know that's hard to understand.

So, what do we do with all these feelings?

I think, perhaps, that we have to use all our sadness and pain to our advantage. That sounds strange, doesn't it? But if you know what it's like to be hurt, to be let down, you will make sure that you don't hurt or let anyone else down.

You can use your pain to heal and forgive. You've been holding on to so much anger, James. Your dad. Your mum. School. Maybe it's time to let it go. Don't let it eat you up. It will fester inside, and you will end up bitter and sad.

And that's just not you. You were born to shine.

Besides, forgiving people doesn't mean you are weak. It doesn't mean everything is forgotten and that they deserve any more of your time or thoughts or worries. No. We forgive people who have wronged us to free _ourselves_. To say to them, you have no more power over me. I am free. I am free from you and the pain you caused me. I am so much more than what you've done to me. Remember, what _you_ think about yourself is the most important thing of all, not what anyone else says or thinks.

Instead, fill your life with art and music and good food and reading and dancing and singing. Find people who love you and want the best for you. Dear friends like Harriet and Joel are hard to find. Just hold tightly on to them with everything you've got. They will become your family, your cheerleaders, your light in the

darkness, and they will help you see how truly
special and wonderful you are.

I wish I could stay with you for ever, but I'm
old and I'm tired and I've had such a wonderful
life. I wish I could see you grow up into the
handsome, fierce, honest and brave man I know
you will be. I wish I could see you fall in love
with whoever you choose, and be at your wedding
someday.

I'll always be with you, and I think a piece of
you will always stay with me. You have changed
me for ever. Always remember the laughter,
and dancing, and fun adventures we have had
together, and just know that I'll be with you, by
your side, championing, supporting and loving
you.

James, you'll Always Be My Baby, my Hero,
and know that I'll see you One Sweet Day.

I love you, my darling, my brave, glittering
grandson.

All my love, for ever,
Nan

When we finish reading the letter, Dad hugs me and
I let him. And then he whispers in my ear, "She loved

you so much. And I love you, James. You need to know that. I'll do better, I promise."

I nestle into his shoulder and I finally, finally let myself cry. Dad holds me until I can't cry any more. We stay like that for a long time, until the shadows lengthen and the silver moonlight creeps through the curtains.

CHAPTER 36

The next morning, I wake up and think, *Oh, it's Mr Hamilton's wedding!*

And then I remember that I'm not going. Once Dad has made up his mind, there's no changing it.

Well, there was once. When I was seven, I wanted a hamster. Like, really, *really* wanted one. Mum and Dad both said no, but I ground them down. I screamed and moaned and groaned, and then I gave them the silent treatment. Dad said he liked it because I was quiet for once.

But I didn't let this put me off! Oh no! When nothing seemed to be working, I made some placards and banners from what I could find in the house and marched up and down the hallway shouting, "What do I want? A HAMSTER! When do I want it? NOW!"

Finally, they gave in and I got a hamster for Christmas.

Somehow, I don't think the same tactics would work this time.

I eat breakfast on my own and try not to think too much about everyone else in the choir going to the wedding. Joel's probably woken up all excited and is doing his hair and getting his smart clothes out. He said he was wearing a tie because it's a wedding and that's what you do, which made me laugh.

As I'm washing up and wondering where Dad is, I get a text and my heart jumps: it's Joel!

Sorry you can't come along today! Will tell you all about it on Monday. Wish you could be there. J

I spend the morning listening to Mariah in my room, and it's a "Lead the Way", "You're Mine", "#Beautiful" kind of morning. I sit at my desk humming along.

To take my mind off the wedding, I start writing a poem for Sandra. It's something I need to do. I need to start making amends.

But soon I find myself imagining what today's wedding will be like. I'm glad the sun is shining for Mr Hamilton and Sam. I imagine them holding hands while yellow and orange leaves tumble from the sky around them. I think maybe they'll have champagne and posh little things to eat – they're called *canapés*, I think – while the choir sings. And then everyone will sit down and they'll have afternoon tea with fancy, delicate sandwiches and scrumptious, delicate cakes. I went for afternoon tea once with Mum and Dad and Nan, and it was so good!

Afterwards, for their first dance, Mr Hamilton and Sam-with-the-silver-hair will twirl and sway to "When I Saw You" by Mariah Carey.

I close my eyes and smile, but instead of Mr Hamilton and Sam dancing, I see—

"James! James!"

It's Dad, and I wonder why he's so excited as he bursts into my room. He's sweating and laughing when he sees how confused I am.

"Where have you been?" I ask, perplexed.

"Just … out … thinking…" He's out of breath, and I think maybe he should *really* have carried on with that 5K running app.

"Come on! Let's go! Didn't you hear me last night?" Dad yells excitedly.

Then he kneels down in front of me, and I think he's finally lost his mind.

"I've been trying so hard to keep you safe, mate," he says, "and I just hate the idea of anyone laughing at you, or being mean to you, like Paul."

"It's OK, Dad," I say, "I understand. I get it." And I *do* get it. He wants to protect me.

"But you can't live like that, can you?" he carries on. "I have to let you … let you go and be you and live your life and … I'll be there for you, mate. I will be, no matter what happens and no matter what you decide. I promise, I will be there."

It's my turn to pat him on the shoulder and say, "OK, Dad. Thanks. That means a lot."

Then I laugh and say, "You can get up now."

He laughs and wipes his nose because it's snotty and I can see he's been crying, and I wonder if I've been wrong about my dad all along.

I stand up as he stands up, and he gives me a hug, but this time he doesn't pat me on the back or make a joke. He just holds me.

Then he breaks away suddenly. "Come on, then, James! You need to get ready, mate!"

"Ready for what?" I say, shaking my head.

He wiggles his body in a very embarrassing way. I think it's his version of dancing? "Stick on some Mariah tunes, son, and let's get ready for this wedding!"

"Are you coming with me, Dad?"

We're both breathless and sweaty from running to the wedding venue. We couldn't find parking nearby so we had to run for ages!

We held hands all the way and I was giddy with excitement.

I have to say that, despite the clammy sweat, I am still looking *fabulous*! Skinny dark blue jeans, my stunning, shiny brogues, and a shimmering, glittering purple shirt that Mum bought me a long time ago.

"Come on, Dad!" I squeal.

"Sorry, mate, I'm not invited, remember? And I don't think I would pass as a choir member!" he says, snickering. "But don't worry, I'll wait out here for you with the other parents."

We're standing outside the venue – it's *so* fancy – and I can see the choir jostling and whispering. There's a group of parents waiting nearby in the car park, and they're all dressed up too!

I can't believe I'm here, and it's finally the day, and Joel will be here too!

"Go on, you'd better get going," Dad says.

I look up at him and whisper, "Love you, Dad."

His eyes crinkle in acknowledgement. "Love you too. Now, go on, I'll be waiting for you here."

I strut over to where the choir are gathered. They're clearly making a big effort to be extra quiet for the surprise, and I wave and smile at everyone – my big entrance!

Mrs Gallagher spots me and her expression is stern. Whoops! She waves me over, and when I approach, she says, "James, I'm sorry, but you don't have permission to be here."

"No, but I do! My dad, he's in the car park, see? He's letting me do this."

She looks over to where Dad is now chatting to Joel's parents, and her mouth twists into a small smile. "Well, let me speak to him to be sure. Wait here, I'll be back in a moment."

She walks over to Dad, and I squeeze in at the back of the choir next to Joel, and can't help laughing when I see his reaction.

"What?! What are you doing here?" he whisper-exclaims.

"My dad changed his mind," I say, giggling. He looks so smart in his tie and white shirt!

Mrs Gallagher comes back and gives me a grin and thumbs up. A few minutes later, we hear cheering and clapping coming from inside, and this must be it! *They're coming!*

A ripple of excitement spreads through the choir.

"Shhh!" says Mrs Gallagher, flapping her hands up and down. "They're coming out now! Listen out for the start of the music and GOOD LUCK!"

The doors open and people are cheering and throwing rose petals at Mr Hamilton and Sam. They're wearing matching electric-blue suits with yellow flowers in their buttonholes. It's so cool to finally see Sam! He has silvery-grey locs and dark skin. They both look like princes at the end of a fairy tale – happy and glowing and so in love. The autumn sun is making their suits shimmer and I watch them laugh and hold hands, greeting all their wedding guests.

Could that be me one day?

I can see that Miss Davies, Mrs Farooq and Miss Clarke and some of the other school staff are there too. It takes a moment to realize that the woman wearing a stunning coral-pink dress and laughing and chatting to everyone is *Miss Wilson*! She looks over at me and I wait for her glare. Instead, she nods, a slight smile on her face.

Kindness and forgiveness, James.

I smile back at Miss Wilson and wave.

See, Nan! I can forgive people.

Everyone's hugging and crying and cheering. I feel so excited and nervous, and even Joel, always so still and calm, is bouncing up and down next to me.

As they move through their guests, Mr Hamilton finally sees us and his hands fly to his face and he looks so surprised and amazed. He breaks out into the biggest smile I've ever seen. He hits Sam's shoulder lightly and whispers something in his ear, and they cuddle and kiss.

The wedding party move forward so everyone's watching us, and Mr Hamilton and Sam come right to the front, holding hands. Mr Hamilton is waving at us all with his other hand and laughing.

Mrs Gallagher starts the music and we begin to sing "Rise Up" by Andra Day. I'm beaming with happiness because this may be as close as I'll ever get to feeling how Mariah feels when she sings the super-amazing high notes in "Emotions". *Bring it on!*

I sing for Mr Hamilton and Sam. And I sing for Ruth and Eliana, and all the people fighting and hoping and dreaming. I sing for Nan. I sing for my mum and dad.

I sing for all the kids out there who know exactly who they are but get told their feelings aren't valid. That their truth, their identity, who they are isn't valid. I also sing for the kids who don't know who they are yet, but will one day.

I sing louder and louder, and it feels glorious and hopeful and joyous and absolutely perfect.

After we've sung our song, Mr Hamilton comes over with Sam.

"Hello, everyone! WOW! I can't believe you're all here!"

They are both smiling widely, and we grin back.

"That was such a marvellous surprise! You sounded AMAZING!"

We all giggle and mutter *thank you, thank you*. It feels weird talking to a teacher outside school!

"This is Sam! The messy one who likes rugby and never tidies up after himself!" Mr Hamilton says as he wraps his arm around Sam's waist.

"I'm not THAT bad!" Sam laughs, giving Mr Hamilton a little push.

"Sam, tell us about Mr Hamilton!" I yell.

"NNNOOOOOOOOOOOOOO!" Mr Hamilton laughs. "Don't you dare!"

"Go on, Sam!" someone else shouts.

"Well, let's see," he says, rubbing his chin. "He's ALWAYS reading! He loves crime thrillers and murder mysteries and watches Poirot and Miss Marple on repeat."

Mr Hamilton laughs and shakes his head, embarrassed.

"Tell us more about Mr Hamilton!" I cheer.

"He loves swimming. He goes swimming three times a week. Sometimes before school, sometimes after. He says it clears his head. His dad used to take him swimming, and so it reminds him of him."

I look at Joel and he's crying and laughing.

"More! What else?" I call out.

"He talks about you kids ALL THE TIME! He's always worrying about you and thinking about how he can make your lessons fun and ALWAYS marking your books! You mean a lot to him."

"MORE!"

"What else? Hmmmmm. Well, now … he's officially my HUSBAND!" Sam yells, and we all cheer and clap.

As the cheers die down and the newlyweds move on to talk to their other guests, Joel turns and looks at me and says matter-of-factly, "Oh, by the way …

I'm gay. I just wanted you to know. To be the first to know."

I smile at him.

I think I knew all this time.

"Thank you for sharing such an important part of yourself with me," I whisper.

He shrugs, like it's nothing at tall. Like he hasn't just been the bravest kid in the world.

"And I'm sorry," I say.

Joel looks up quizzically and says, "Sorry?"

"Not about you being gay, of course! That's cool. It's great! But I'm sorry about … me not being there for you. At all. Not one little bit. I should have been there for you. To talk to. You've been trying to tell me for ages, haven't you?"

"It's OK," Joel says, and he closes his eyes. "Everything's OK, honestly. You've had a rubbish time recently, and it's no big deal, no big thing. I just felt like I needed to tell you."

He screws his eyes tight shut now and he's blushing and grinning.

I say, "Thank you," and then I say, "I'm really proud of you."

With the sun behind him, Joel seems to be glittering and gleaming, like his smile has lit him up.

It's such a big, open, happy smile, and I wonder how anyone could say this is wrong, that he is wrong, that I am wrong, that we are wrong.

We stand there, side by side, and I don't ever want this moment to end.

On the way home, Dad and I stop at Nan's house and we stand there for a long time. I realize that we've only talked about getting the house ready and getting the funeral over with. We haven't talked about *her*, not really.

"She loved a wedding, your nan," Dad says.

"I remember when she had too much sherry at Auntie Kathy and Weird Bruce's wedding and had everyone on the dance floor," I say, giggling.

"She had all the moves," says Dad, laughing along. "I reckon that's where you get your dancing from, your nan. Definitely not me!"

It's nice just to laugh with Dad again and remember Nan. She meant so much to us.

"I want to talk about her, Dad," I say gently but assertively. He nods, and I carry on. "And I want to talk about Joel and school and Mr Hamilton and everything that's happening with me."

"And I want you to do that too, James. I know I'm

not very good at talking sometimes, but I will try and be better."

"Even better at cooking?" I tease.

He laughs and ruffles my hair.

We stand there, watching Nan's house and remembering. Remembering all the laughing and dancing and meals together. Remembering the quiet nights watching TV and munching on sweets and chocolate. Remembering the times I stayed the night and I felt so special. Remembering when Dad and Nan and I would sit outside in the garden drinking tea and listening to the birds sing and the leaves rustle, and we didn't have to speak because we were there with each other.

I'm suddenly aware that there's something yapping and biting at my feet – it's Princess! Oh, I *love* this little thing! I crouch down and stroke her. She farts excitedly, and then leaps up into my arms, licking me and biting at my ears.

"Hello, James, how are you?" Ruth asks, walking up to us.

"I'm good, thanks. It was Mr Hamilton's wedding today and we – the choir – sang at it!"

"That sounds lovely! And you must be James's dad?" says Eliana, smiling at him.

"Erm … yes … that's me," says Dad gruffly, and he shakes both their hands.

"How are you both doing?" Ruth asks, her brow creasing in sympathy.

"We're good, thank you. Well, we will be," says Dad. "And I wanted to say … erm … *thank you* for checking in on Mum and, erm … looking after her."

"Our pleasure," says Eliana warmly. She seems to have relaxed a little, like something's changed between them.

"And thank you for looking after me too," I say, giving them each a great big hug.

"Any time, James," Eliana whispers into my ear. I let her go and I'm grinning now.

"Anyway, we'll leave you to it," says Ruth. "Come on, Princess. Nice to see you again, James."

We say goodbye, and as they walk away I realize they're holding hands again. It's good to see.

We turn back to Nan's house.

"Joel told me he was gay today," I say to Dad quietly.

There's a pause.

I wait.

"Good for him, I'm really pleased for him, mate," Dad says.

He puts an arm around me.

"Thanks, Dad," I say.

We stay there for a long time – I'm not sure *how* long – until Dad declares, "Come on, it's getting late! Do you want to ask Joel and Harriet if they want to come over tonight for a film?"

I squeal with excitement and say, "Errr ... yes! We can watch *Glitter*!"

"Is that a Mariah Carey film?" says Dad, laughing and shaking his head.

"Of course! And there's A LOT of history around this film. Do you want to hear about it?"

"Sure," says Dad.

I turn around and blow a kiss at Nan's house.

She's not there any more, and that's OK. She's with me now, all the time, tucked safely in my memories.

And then Dad and I walk home, hand in hand, laughing and talking.

<u>What Are The Hardest Words To Say?</u>

I'M SORRY.

PLEASE FORGIVE ME.

PLEASE COME BACK HOME, MUM.

GAY.
GAY.
GAY.

I LIKE YOU.
I LOVE YOU!
LEAVE ME ALONE!
I DON'T DESERVE THIS.

EVERYTHING WILL BE OK, DAD.
I'M PROUD OF YOU, SON.

No, the hardest words to say are:

I MISS YOU.
GOODBYE, FOR NOW.

CHAPTER 37

"Hi, Sandra?"

Sandra looks up at me from the table. There's only one week left before we break up for the half-term holiday and the canteen is loud and chaotic. There are midday assistants running around, cutting up food for reception children and mopping up spilled water and dropped food and cajoling moody, crying kids to eat their lunches.

"Oh, hi, James! How are you?" Sandra says. Her Year 5 friends ignore me and carry on talking.

"I'm good, thanks," I say, bright red in the face and *totally* embarrassed. But this is something I need to do, and have wanted to do for a long time. "I wanted to give you this, it's a poem I wrote. It's to say thank you for when you came over and chatted to me about my nan."

Sometimes we're so wrapped up in our own problems and worries that we forget that other people are struggling too. And Sandra was sad about her little cat Lola, but she *still* came over to me in the playground to make sure I was OK. And that means a lot.

Because kindness makes us stronger.

I hand her a piece of folded paper. It's not much, and it's not some super-cool present, but it's all I have to say thank you.

It says:

<u>Lola</u>

Lola is sleek and black as night.
Her eyes glitter and gleam in starlight.
Moonlight sparkles on her soft, smooth fur.
She waits outside the window watching over you.
Remembering, dreaming, purring.
Creeping, stalking, pouncing through the silence.
When morning scatters sunlit diamonds
across the lawn
She vanishes.
Just a dream, a memory,
Safely tucked inside your heart.

Sandra looks taken aback and whispers, "Thank you, James. Is it OK if I read it when I'm on my own?"

"Of course! Anyway, I should go. We're going to put on a dance show in the playground. Come along if you want!"

She nods, grasps my hand for a moment, and then slips my poem into her dress pocket.

I walk outside. The autumn sun is shining and the playground is full of laughter and screeching.

I see Paul glaring at me. He's on his own now.

What would Mariah Carey do?

What would Marsha P. Johnson do?

What would my nan do?

What would James do?

Paul looks around for someone – anyone – to laugh at me with.

But no one's there. Something has changed in our class, in our school and I can't help but wonder: maybe I've changed too?

So, I shrug and I turn away from him. I've spent enough time and energy worrying about him, what he thinks, what he might do. From now on, I'll focus on the people who deserve it, the people who care about me and the people I care about.

Beginning Again

I begin again.
I pick myself up after you
Tore me down.
I don't blame you.
I don't even think of you.
A spark inside of me
Once extinguished by you
Burns brightly once more.

Now that's a pretty good one, isn't it? I could almost imagine a famous, fabulous diva singing it someday...

I see Joel chatting to some of the other boys in our class.

He comes racing over and asks, "Are we going to have a boogie and a dance, then?"

"Don't say boogie, please!" I say drily, then pretend-shudder and laugh.

Together we cross the playground, and I see Nathan sitting on the bench talking to Jake and showing him his comic books. His face is animated and he looks happy and relaxed.

He looks up and sees me and I wave, because, well,

you know, we've been through a lot. Nathan waves back shyly.

Joel and I wander over to Harriet and Ameera, who are already dancing and leaping about the playground. Rafe, Harry, Ohrim, Summer and Anna all join in, and some younger children are watching and cheering.

We're choreographing a dance to Mariah Carey's frankly brilliant song "Make It Happen". It's about believing in yourself, taking control of your life and getting back up every time you fall down.

It's perfect.

I look at Harriet really going for it and laugh when she trips and tries to make it look like it's part of the routine.

"Ready?" Joel says.

I take a big, deep breath, grin at Joel, and say, "I'm *so* ready. Let's go!"

JAMES AND JOEL'S ✦ QUIZZES ✦

So, as you know, Joel and I worked really hard on our presentation about Marsha P. Johnson. Well, Joel definitely did. I sulked for a lot of it. But anyhoo! I thought I'd show you some of the quizzes and information we included in our AMAZING presentation because this is my story and I can do what I want! Ha!

You could try to work out the answers on your own, or with a family member, or as a class. You could get someone to photocopy them and draw lines to match them up or colour-code them if you're super fancy!

Have fun and stay FABULOUS!

QUIZ 1

What does LGBTQ+ mean? Match the terms on this page to their definitions on the next!

Terms:

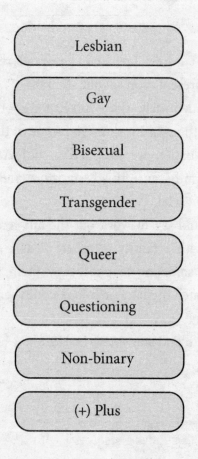

Lesbian

Gay

Bisexual

Transgender

Queer

Questioning

Non-binary

(+) Plus

Definitions:

People who are attracted to more than one gender

People whose gender identity and/or sexual orientation is not included in the letters LGBT

Women who are attracted to women

Men who are attracted to men

People whose gender doesn't fit into the categories of "man" or "woman". They might use "Mx" (pronounced "mix" or "mux") instead of "Mr" or "Mrs" and "they" instead of "he" or "she"

Word used by people to describe themselves if they are exploring or unsure about their sexual identity and/or gender identity, or to avoid applying a social label to themselves

This broad term can be used to celebrate all gender identity and sexual orientations

People whose gender does not fit with the sex they were assigned at birth

This next quiz was really tricky! Most of the kids in our class knew about Elton John, but they didn't know many of these other trailblazers from the LGBTQ+ community! How well will you do?

QUIZ 2

Match the famous person to their description!

Person:

Stormé DeLarverie

Billie Jean King

Audre Lorde

Harvey Milk

Simon Nkoli

Barbara Gittings

Lady Phyll

RuPaul

Description:

Writer who described herself as "black, lesbian, mother, warrior, poet" who used her poems to fight sexism, racism, and homophobia

Anti-apartheid leader and gay activist in South Africa who fought for freedom and equality

American gay politician, activist and visionary who was murdered in 1978

One of the most successful American drag queens in history and also a pop star and actor

Co-founder of UK Black Pride, who works with Kaleidoscope Trust to fight for LGBTQ+ rights around the world

Famous tennis player who has dedicated her life to fighting for gender equality

Referred to as the mother of the LGBT civil rights movement, who worked to change the view of homosexuality as being a mental illness

Many think she started the Stonewall riots, also known as the "guardian of lesbians" because she was a volunteer street patrol worker

ANSWERS

QUIZ 1

(Lesbian)   Women who are attracted to women

(Gay)   Men who are attracted to men

(Bisexual)   People who are attracted to more than one gender

(Transgender)   People whose gender does not fit with the sex they were assigned at birth

(Queer)   This broad term can be used to celebrate all gender identities and sexual orientations

(Questioning)   Word used by people to describe themselves if they are exploring or unsure about their sexual identity and/or gender identity, or to avoid applying a social label to themselves

(Non-binary)   People whose gender doesn't fit into the categories of "man" or "woman". They might use "Mx" instead of "Mr" or "Mrs" and "they" instead of "he" or "she"

(+) Plus   People whose gender identity and/or sexual orientation is not included in the letters LGBT

QUIZ 2

Stormé DeLarverie   Many think she started the Stonewall riots; also known as the "guardian of lesbians" because she was a volunteer street patrol worker

Billie Jean King   Famous tennis player who has dedicated her life to fighting for gender equality

Audre Lorde   Writer who described herself as "black, lesbian, mother, warrior, poet" who used her poems to fight sexism, racism, and homophobia

Harvey Milk   American gay politician, activist and visionary who was murdered in 1978

Simon Nkoli

Anti-apartheid leader and gay activist in South Africa who fought for freedom and equality

Barbara Gittings

Referred to as the mother of the LGBT civil rights movement, who worked to change the view of homosexuality as being a mental illness

Lady Phyll

Co-founder of UK Black Pride, who works with Kaleidoscope Trust to fight for LGBTQ+ rights around the world

RuPaul

One of the most successful American drag queens in history and also a pop star and actor

A NOTE FROM IAN EAGLETON

School can be tough. Life can be tough.

When I was a kid, I was quiet and gentle. I loved singing, dancing and writing stories about mermaids. But I soon learned that, according to some people, little boys shouldn't behave like this.

When I began secondary school, the other boys in my year immediately decided that I was gay. That everything about me was gay and therefore I was made a target. I was bullied terribly, and I spent all of my time at school being terrified. I was spat at, ignored, whispered about and vilified. People refused to look at me or speak to me.

I had a few friends who tried hard to look after me,

but I spent a lot of time hiding in the library, which is where I discovered a love of books. How wonderful it was to escape into different worlds and become someone else.

The only problem was that there were no LGBTQ+ characters in any of the stories I read. I felt left out and excluded.

When I left university, I became a primary school teacher and was sad to see homophobic bullying take place in my classroom. It brought back all those terrible years for me. I decided to do something about it and began writing books that featured LGBTQ+ relationships and characters for my class. At this point, I was just enjoying writing and couldn't see it going anywhere. No one wanted to publish my books! People kept telling me that kids didn't need LGBTQ+ inclusive books.

I was close to giving up.

But, when my husband and I started going through the adoption process and knew we were going to adopt a little baby boy, the need for LGBTQ+ inclusive books became even more important. I wanted our son to see families like his in the books he read.

So, I picked my pencil up and began writing again.

For me. For my son. For all the LGBTQ+ kids and teenagers, and even adults, out there who have never seen themselves in books.

My first picture book to be published is called *Nen and the Lonely Fisherman*, and it's illustrated by James Mayhew. It's a hopeful, gay fairy tale. I have also written a book about overcoming anxiety called *Violet's Tempest*, illustrated by Clara Anganuzzi. This book also features a gay couple!

I have lots of other LGBTQ+ inclusive books coming out, but *Glitter Boy* is my debut middle-grade novel. As you've read, it's a story about anger and bullying and resentment. Of not feeling like you can be yourself.

It recognizes that school can be tough. That life can be tough.

But it also recognizes that life for people in the LGBTQ+ community can be full of love, hope, resilience, bravery and joy. That we deserve happiness, safety and respect.

But most importantly, Glitter Boy is about allowing yourself to shine and sparkle and never giving up, even when the darkness seems to be drawing in around you.

ACKNOWLEDGEMENTS

There are so many people to thank, with so many people involved in the magical process of creating a book.

Firstly, thank you to my editor, Linas Alsenas. He saw the potential in a picture-book manuscript I sent to him and encouraged me to try writing a middle-grade novel, which eventually became *Glitter Boy*. Without his belief in me, his passion, dedication, and conscientious, thoughtful work on the story, this book would not exist.

Thank you also to the whole team at Scholastic – I am so proud to be publishing my debut middle-grade novel with you.

Thank you to Sarah Dutton and her team of copyeditors and proofreaders, who have helped shape and streamline James's story. Your hard work and diligence is really appreciated. Thank you also to Jada Lightning.

Thank you to Melissa Chaib and Sarah Baldwin for the BEAUTIFUL cover illustrations and design. The book looks so colourful, eye-catching and joyful, and the cover captures the themes of the story perfectly.

Thank you to publicist Hannah Love and the marketing team for their hard work behind the scenes promoting *Glitter Boy*. You are all brilliant!

To the rest of the Scholastic family – thank you so much for helping me create and share such a special story with readers everywhere. Your efforts and talents have not gone unnoticed!

Thank you to the incredibly talented children's poet Julie Anna Douglas, who allowed me to use one of her beautiful poems as a starting off point for James's cat-themed poem.

A massive thank you to all the booksellers, independent bookshops, teachers and friends on Twitter, book bloggers and school librarians who have been there for me since the very beginning. You're brilliant!

A big warm hug and thank-you to the Eagleton family – I wrote a novel! I can't believe it! Whilst some of James's experiences are based on my own, I have been very lucky to have wonderful parents and brothers. My brothers now have families of their own, and I love them all very much too.

Thank you to the Newland clan for your warmth,

kindness and love. It's great to be part of your family as well.

Grandparents are an important part of this story, and I was blessed to have loving, amazing grandparents who would have done anything for me. Much love also goes to AJ, who is such a special part of our family.

A big shout out to all my friends: far too many to list! How lucky am I to have such caring, funny, supportive people in my life, many of whom have been my friends since I was twelve, when I discovered a local drama group?

Thank you to my little family: my husband and my son. You are the reason I get up every morning and the reason I write. I love you both very much and am so grateful for your unconditional love.

And finally, a thank you to you, reader! Thank you for taking the time to share James's journey of self-discovery. I hope you take with you some of James's bravery and strength. I hope the book also reminds you that you are fabulous! Never allow anyone to dim your light – keep glittering brightly!